Pockets of Interlude

Zahra Jessa

Cover art:

Ayanna Henry
&
Zahra Jessa

This being human is a guest house.
Every morning a new arrival.

A joy, a depression, a meanness,
some momentary awareness comes
as an unexpected visitor.

Welcome and entertain them all!
Even if they're a crowd of sorrows,
who violently sweep your house
empty of its furniture,
still, treat each guest honourably.
He may be clearing you out
for some new delight.

The dark thought, the shame, the malice,
meet them at the door laughing,
and invite them in.

Be grateful for whoever comes,
because each has been sent
as a guide from beyond.

    -   Rumi

MESSAGE

I created pockets of interlude as an ode to how much words have taught me. They've taught me to be kind, patient, loving. They've taught me compassion.
Most of all, they've taught me the importance of creativity.
Life as we know it can go so wrong in so many ways, and we all have our ways of coping. Of coming back to ourselves after long days, days we get lost in the maze we call society. When we come home and let ourselves breathe.
I hope these stories provide you with a smile, a feeling or a spark of hope.
I hope they help you breathe.

For my rose:
Thank you for guiding me through every single chapter, thank you for reading every word.
Thank you for being my rock, my biggest fan.
Thank you for being my best friend.
I wouldn't have been able to do this without you.

For my family:
For the unending, unconditional love.
For being proud of me.

CONTENTS

Message

1

LAY THE HEART

Sand, unbreathable dust tucked on the marble entries of every brown bricked and sloped house, travelling through the dunes with a fierce, unrelenting drift. It was a usual day for the Goddess of mortality, who slouched on her marble throne, hoping to get some repose before the next mortal entered her realm.

Ma'at gazed at the frames hanging off the walls, vibrant paintings of all the gods and goddesses that had existed before her. Of all the families that held the universe's fragile power in the palm of their hands, the creases in them mapping out the farcical, delicate philosophy called destiny. Ma'at had no mother, suffering solemnly to hold back verbalising the misfortune that stemmed from this absence when conversing and complying with her father's great demands. He never let her speak about it, so she kept it buried, gently prodding at the base of her heart. She missed her mother dearly, oddly enough as she never knew the woman and hoped for one every night of her naive youth, praying and begging for some sort of sign that she existed.

None came, and Ma'at's pining and fascination ultimately dampened as she grew, faced with the obligation of the wings her father brought to life and made aching slashes across the soft skin on her back to place them there. Then once the wounds had healed, a feather had fallen from her, called the feather of truth. The feather glowed, and all the immortals loved it, but Ma'at did not; she almost despised it. The feather, in all its glory, merely devised a miserable plan for the beginning of the rest of her eternal life. It demanded things from her she was unwilling to give, heartbreaks she had never recovered from, and a feeling of sorrow deep at the base of her chest, prodding her heart every chance it got.

Ma'at was a spiritual symbol, but she also had a physical embodiment. She was part human, as her father had demanded she be for her to fully understand the hefty job of scrutinising mortality. She felt misunderstood among the immortals, among their vigorous stipulations. But she never felt human, either. She never felt like she belonged, not truly.

Her eyes fluttered shut, but the bell came too soon. The sound of another dead mortal. She slouched in her chair until she heard the door squeak, and a human was hauled in, confused and horrified. She always tried to be kind to them, as some had no idea of the reality of their existence. The triviality of it. Ma'at rose, and her white dress followed her every curve from the waist down, her wings spread out behind her, mighty and striking. They were a statement of all the power she wore like a crown, balancing on her head the jewels that could change the fate of the universe.

Atop her head, she wore a nemes with a single ostrich feather that stood horizontally, fluttering in the breeze that slithered in through the slightly ajar window. She wore a sheath with golden straps on her chest, and her flat, toned belly was wrapped in thin gold bands of nitid jewellery. The human looked up at her with wide eyes. Her green eyes glowed, and her beauty shimmered in the natural light.

Her father made her physical body beautiful, so the mortals could gaze at her and find a semblance of peace in their last moments before the next life. He had said her beauty had encompassed the entire universe in one half-mortal. Ma'at rarely felt beautiful, however. How could she, when she had sent so many mortals to a dark hole where no beauty was to be found?

"Lay the heart." She spoke, demanding and powerful. Once the human came close enough, Forina, the heart bearer, brought the heart out and placed it on the golden tainted scale, and Ma'at rose from her chair as Forina scurried away with blood-stained hands. Four servants scampered, carrying the golden box with the feather of truth, and lay it on the stone next to the scale. Anubis then emerged from the shadows and glared at Ma'at.

The two had never gotten along, but Anubis came when he was summoned. It was his job, after all. She nodded at him, and he placed the feather on the scale, and the scale tipped to the heart. The heart was heavier, meaning the mortal could not find peace in the journey to come, and the heart was to be fed to the fierce monster that lay locked behind the mighty doors at the end of the hall.

Ma'at sighed, and her eyes fluttered shut. She thought it might feel better with every mortal that didn't pass the test; she thought she might get used to it. But she never did.

With a flick of her finger, the human was taken by the guards on either side of him, and Ma'at whispered a prayer for him under her breath. She knew it would not help, but it had become a habit.

"Your duty is over," Anubis said, with an attitude that leaked in his tone. She sighed, relieved, as her handmaiden helped her down the gold steps. "It amazes me how you still can't walk down the steps yourself." he added.

"It amazes me how you haven't yet figured out how to put a stop to the nonsense that spills from your mouth." Her handmaiden, Sarina, huffed and gave Ma'at a wide smile as she rolled her eyes. Ma'at chuckled and reached for her hand.

After Sarina had drawn a bath for her and scrubbed her body of all evil, sitting behind her on the marble and rubbing the cloth over her back in soothing circles, she lay against Sarina's thigh and her eyes fell shut. When her skin had soaked all the natron from the water, and she smelt like perfume, Sarina wrapped her in silk and guided her to the comforting sheets of her bed.

"Come," Ma'at said, and Sarina sat shyly on the edge of the bed. Ma'at tapped and Sarina lay her head on the pillow, facing her. "You're so beautiful," Sarina spoke gently. "And I know you despise when people ramble about your physical features, but that is not what I refer to." Sarina then placed her hand on Ma'at's chest. "I refer to what lays under your ribs."

Ma'at smiled, knowing Sarina was ignorant of her words' value. Ma'at, although it was forbidden, let Sarina sleep next to her, knowing her lover would not come to her bed that night. She felt a love for her she could not fully explain.

In the orange hue of the dawn the following day, Ma'at found her peace. She had just completed her duties for the morning and let her skin darken outside in the sun until Sarina had willed her to come back into the shade, giving her scriptures to read in hopes of occupying her mind. She had lost interest and resorted to staring mindlessly out of her window. Her father had made this realm look like what some now call ancient Egypt. She loved to watch the dust and sand moving through the city, the old structures of the brick houses and the coloured pots and vases that lay limp. The people that made it feel somewhat real, busy with their lives, selling their goods in the markets and constantly haggling for more.

She knew very well that this realm was a replica of the real thing, almost a hoax, but Ma'at never fixated on that fact. She often enjoyed the blue hue in the sky and the little green birds that would land on her balcony, chirping sweet melodies and plucking the feathers from their backs.

"My love, are your duties completed?" Thoth said softly behind her as if not to frighten her with his presence. Ma'at turned to him, gazing up at him lovingly. Thoth was the god of wisdom and her other half. He was moulded for her, which Ma'at thought made their love fickle at first, but she had grown to like how well he treated her.

She spread her arms out for him, and his eyes turned wide, misty with love as he kneeled in front of her. He chuckled, laying his head on her shoulder and kissing her neck as she ran her fingers through his soft, curly hair. He seemed to know what she was feeling.

"That bad?" he said.

She nodded, and he wrapped his arms around her. They lay back together on the bed, and he lifted his weight off her with his arms, his eyes journeying around her face.

"I feel like I need some sort of reprieve. This feather is sucking all the energy out of me."

"Would you like to escape to Earth?"

She scoffed, and rolled her eyes. "I'm sure that would make it worse."

He nodded, patiently nodding as she spoke of all her burdens. Eventually, he stopped her words with a kiss. The human condition was phenomenal in this way, where one could use their bodies to speak to each other. She kissed him back, and let his hands roam her skin.

A harsh knock on the door interrupted them.

"Your duties are demanded."

She sighed, and Thoth released her from under him, standing and offering her his hand. "I'll walk you."

His fingers wrapped around hers, and he squeezed.

Her duties felt like days of turmoil, and she would wait for the last mortal with the constant tapping of her foot. Finally, it came, and Ma'at knew it was different from the moment he entered. This mortal was not afraid nor confused. He seemed almost fascinated, his eyes gawking at the walls of paintings and the red rug under his feet that led up to the scale. Ma'at watched as his eyes finally landed on the feather, and then he did something Ma'at had never seen. He started to laugh, almost manically.

She called Sarina over to her. "Do you know who this is?"

The lines between her brows darkened as she shook her head. "Why do you ask?"

"He seems-- different."

"I'll find out."

Sarina returned a few seconds later. "Among Earth, he was known to be a wizard."

Ma'at felt her heartbeat quicken. She had heard about the power that rested on Earth; small bits of immortality had escaped her father, landing on Earth as powerful rocks. The humans that found these rocks knew great power. If this human were a wizard, he would probably stir up trouble.

She gestured for her guards. With a flick of her finger, the human was restrained. Ma'at stood, and the human smiled.

"Ma'at, is it? I've heard about you."

"You have, have you?"

He nodded. "Your beauty troubles you. Your wings, a sign of great freedom, lock you up in your own head."

Ma'at was angered, and her anger leaked from her eyes and locked her jaw as she rose from her throne. She saw Sarina from the corner of her eye, walking to her heedfully. She lifted her hand, and Sarina halted in her tracks.

She drew closer to the human kneeling in front of her. "I pity you." She spoke.

"You pity I found a hint of what you have up here? Do you know what it's like down there? Have you ever once visited the mess your father created on Earth? The tragedy and the war, and all the misery. You feel pain for us; I know you do. Because our pain is your pain. You're the mother of humans, the one half-mortal to ever exist. But the thing your father created is wretched."

"My father created love."

"No, your father created hate. There was no such thing before him."

"He is the god of creation, and you will not speak badly of him before me."

"Do you not despise him?"

The question struck Ma'at, and her anger rose to her chest, making it difficult to breathe, but only because some part of him was right.

"Love comes with hate; good comes with the bad. Balance is what my father created, and he was right in doing so." Ma'at's voice echoed in the halls.

"No, a balance should have been created; what your father created was good for some and bad for others. And then he created you to be the judge of that. To carry all the injustices along with you. And it worked, did it not? You feel the pain in us every day. Is it not unfair?"

Ma'at's shaky breaths were not concealable anymore, and she looked the human in the eye. "It is."

The gasps were heard all over the hall. "But it's also what has to happen. It cannot be altered."

"No," the human agreed. "But it can be avenged."

Ma'at took a breath in and turned away from him, making her way back to her throne.

"Lay the heart," she spoke. "Let us see how much of this mortal is redeemable."

The mortal chuckled as Forina brought the heart out to the scale. Anubis gently removed the feather and placed it on the scale. The hall grew quiet, but the silence was deafening as all eyes lay stagnant on the scale as it tipped from side to side. Not even the sound of a single inhale was heard. The scale was not making a decision, perpetually tipping from one side to another.

Then, Ma'at felt it. A sharp pain in her chest shot up and out through her feathers. She cried out in pain and grasped her chest. Sarina rushed to her, holding her weight with both arms. Ma'at felt legless, and the pain made her legs wobble. They both tumbled to the floor, and the mortal started to laugh, and he did not stop until the guards dragged him from the hall.

"What's wrong?" Sarina wailed, holding on to Ma'at's face as she sunk to the floor. The pain was too much to bear; Ma'at held onto Sarina as if she was to die. "It hurts," Ma'at said, her voice strained and trembling. She had never felt this weak.

Then, the scale stopped tipping but did not lean to one side. Instead, it stood perfectly still. It felt like a nightmare, but she saw it in slow motion. The feather of truth lit up in flames, and the hall went into a frenzy almost immediately. Some immortals wept, and some attempted to stop the fire. But all the attempts were fruitless. The fire grew, and Ma'at felt the pain coarse through her body in waves.

"Ma'at," Sarina exclaimed. "Your wings."

Her wings were on fire, and Sarina ran to the shelf where the knives lay and returned with equal parts eagerness and fear spread across the lines of her face.

"No, you can't."

"I don't have a choice," Sarina remarked, and the pain seeped into Ma'at's chest as Sarina started to cut the flaming wings off, and then all she saw was black. Ma'at had never experienced such darkness.

And even when she opened her eyes three days later, it never left. Her father stood over her, anger in his eyes and hate in the clench of his fists.

"What did you do?"

She groaned and held her head. It felt different; she felt different. Ma'at glared up at her father, cold in her eyes. "I did not *do* anything." She said, suddenly having thihs urge to challenge her father. "Father, why did you create the universe?"

He was taken aback. "Have some respect."

"No," Ma'at said. "Answer me."

He sighed. "I created the universe for my pleasure, and I did the same with you. Then, I created injustice, hate and pain."

His words should have burnt a hole through Ma'at's heart, but Ma'at felt nothing. She looked into her father's eyes and felt only hate. "Why?"

"Did I need a reason? I have power and can do what I want with it."

"Then why create love? Remorse? Why create me?"

"I did not create you," he spoke.

"What?"

"You were created when I was bathing in the water of Nun. You were created as a consequence of my actions, as a consequence of chaos."

Ma'at, once again, felt nothing. She had seen the remnants of her wings lying on the side of her bed. She eyed them and then her father. He came close enough to her and whispered. "You are not my daughter, and now that you have no wings, you are nothing. Since your fascination has led you to this," he scoffed. "You will go live among the mortals. And feel everything I've created down there as your own."

Her father left, and the next time she woke up with groggy eyes, Sarina's hands were in hers. Her smile widened when Ma'at scrunched her eyes in pain and managed to gaze back at her.

"Are you okay?"

Ma'at shook her head and tried to find the feeling of love that she once felt for the girl sitting in front of her. She could not. She felt nothing.

Sarina sat closer to her and pushed her hair back. "It's okay. It'll be okay."

"Sarina?" she asked. "I need you to do something for me."

"Anything." Sarina said.

"I need you to go into my father's room and take the knife that lies at his bedside. I need you to bring it to me."

"What? The knife that can kill immortality?"

Ma'at nodded and held Sarina's hand tighter. "Please." She said, "I need you to trust me."

Sarina hesitated but obliged.

Ma'at was compelled. She had no other way to explain it. Once her hands had touched the knife and Sarina had fallen asleep next to her, she slipped out from her covers and made her way through the corridors. The night was dark, and the palace was dead silent.

She saw him lying on his side, with the face and body of her father. But he was not her father.

She gripped the dripping knife tighter beside her, and kneeled on the floor next to him. Watching as his chest fell and rose, she let herself observe him in this vulnerable state. The guards outside his door were already dead. Now he would be too.

She lifted the knife and brought it to his neck. He awoke, his eyes fierce with fear. Watching the bobbing of his throat, Ma'at smiled.

"Ma'at," he pleaded. "It's me; it's your father. Please."

He had terror sitting in his eyes, and the thought brought Ma'at peace. "I don't care." She said, and then watched as she slid the knife across his throat, blood dripping, staining the sheets below him. As he gasped and choked for air, Ma'at dropped the knife beside his bed and walked away.

In the morning, when they had found his body, Ma'at was lying in her sheets, Sarina cuddled up against her and Thoth at her bedside.

There was one more thing she had to do. She asked Thoth to cover her duties when he awoke, and he complied when she told him what had happened to her father.

"Don't worry," he said, running his fingers across her cheek. "You need to grieve."

He left her, and she reached for the blade she sneaked in at night from her bedside. Sarina was still sleeping, innocent of what was to come. But as soon as Ma'at had gripped the blade, Sarina stirred awake.

"Hi," Sarina spoke softly, and Ma'at concealed the blade under the covers once again.

"Hi." Ma'at said back. Sarina smiled, and Ma'at felt a pang. She could not do it when Sarina was looking at her. "Go back to sleep."

"No, it's okay," Sarina said and moved to stretch her body. Ma'at knew if she left the room, she would find out what she had done. So she needed to do it now. "Would you like some water?"

"No." Ma'at said. "I would like to bathe."

Sarina obliged, and walked over to undress Ma'at. She started to remove the rope, her deft fingers working them off rapidly. After she was bare, Ma'at took her hand. "I would like you to bathe with me."

Sarina stilled but nodded.

The bath water was warm, and Ma'at had hidden the blade under her silk robe on the edge of the bath.

"Come." Ma'at spread her arms out, and Sarina slipped into them, Sarina's bare back against Ma'ats chest. She took the damp cloth and started to rub down her neck, to her shoulders in slow circles. When Sarina relaxed against her, she took the blade in her other hand, and placed it on her neck in one quick move. She had meant to instantly slide it across Sarina's neck, but her body could not oblige. Sarina stilled, gasped and then her breath faltered.

"Don't move," Ma'at whispered.

"Ma'at?" Sarina said in a soft trembling voice. Then, she turned toward her. The blade was still scraping across her neck when their eyes met.

Neither of them moved, but Ma'at could not complete the act.

Then, she felt it. The pain was back, spreading across her chest like a fire. It hurt like it had the day her wings burnt up. Everything came back, and Ma'at felt it all at once. The realisation had hit her, and she struggled to breathe as the blade fell into the waters. She leaned onto Sarina and heard her faded voice like she was far away. Then, it all went black.

When she returned to the light, the first thing that returned to her was that she had killed her father and had almost killed Sarina. It felt like a dream, but it was not. The metal around her wrists rubbed against her skin, leaving her with stained skin and pain that was unfamiliar. She was almost bare, scraps of clothes covering her body. Only servants would wear the clothes she was wearing.

When her view became clear, she figured out where she was. The red carpet at her knees led to the scale, and Ma'at saw the blurry paintings on the wall slightly clearer when she lifted the heavy weight of her head.

On the marble throne in the distance sat a girl unrecognisable. Her familiar brown locks were tied up into a bun clipped with shiny jewels. A white dress hovered from her waist, bringing out her mighty curves. The gold bands that had once wrapped around Ma'ats waist now wrapped around hers.

Ma'at finally met her gaze, trembling and afraid she might be correct in her assumption.

She was.

"Lay the heart." Sarina spoke, her voice echoing through the halls, mightier and more powerful than she'd ever heard.

2

YELLOW DANCED IN HIS EYES

"Love is everything." Zayan's grandfather spoke in whispers.

His grandfather's voice echoed in his mind, and Zayan felt them in colours. He pictured what they might look like. If voices were soft, did they look different from how they felt? If his grandfather's voice was alive in his eyes, would they not feel like warm vanilla or decadent hot chocolate? Creeping exquisitely into his body and enlightening it with soothing warmth.

"Why?" Zayan whispered into the space between them.
"Well, it is a lifeline, is it not?"
"What's a lifeline?"
"Something you hold onto. Even if everything goes wrong, love will always be there."

The cold biting winds travelled through the city, and Zayan sat up in his makeshift tent on the hardwood floor, his legs folded, tucked into each other like the beginning of a pretzel. His grandfather's hands were on his, the skin frail and crinkly, like his after a long bath. He kept running his fingers over them, almost to remind him he was still there. He wondered how he would look. If Zayan opened his eyes and could see, how would his grandfather's face react to his sight?

"Do you know why the world is as it is?" his grandfather said.

He shook his head then.

"Well, it all started with a curse. A long, long time ago. A curse placed on humankind as a lesson or a punishment. No one knows which."

Zayan was not a normal child; he saw with his heart. When the night came for him to be born, his mother's wails were heard in the forests, where animals could not sleep. When Zayan was born, his grandmother died.

"Before, the world had billions of humans, and most could see, smell and hear just fine."

"And then what happened?"

"The curse was unforgiving, and humans would suddenly die. Millions a day. A higher power called 'surge' had decided humans should no longer roam the Earth. But the King pleaded and begged and prayed for one more chance, so surge decided humans could live on the rule that no new life would occur. If one was to live, another was to die. If one wanted sight, another would be blind. If one wanted to hear, another would be deaf."

"So this is why I'm unable to see?"

"Yes, your grandmother never had sight, so when you were born, and the higher powers chose her to die, there was no sight to give."

"So if someone new is born, who dies?"

"That is not known. The surge decides who dies. That is why we must live every day as if it is our last. I know you cannot see, but Zayan, you can feel. And the heart is the most powerful force of nature, so feel with your heart, and don't ever stop. They say the curse can be broken only by the purest of heart."

Zayan thought his grandfather was the wisest man ever to live, and that night, Zayan slept against his chest, lulled by the lub-dub inside his chest.

He awoke in the morning with his heart on his sleeve and went in search of his mother. His mother, who he heard from the other room, and used her voice as a guide. He knew the inside of these walls better than anything, he knew where the frames were hung and where the books had been neatly tucked. His mother had guided his hands to them, and Zayan memorised the way each wall felt on his fingertips. If it felt rough, or smooth or somewhere in between.

"Zayan, breakfast."

He used his fingers to glide over the walls and into the rougher dipped edges of the entrance of the kitchen. Then his hands were held, and he was pulled into his seat.

"Hi, my love." his mother said, and he felt her lips on his forehead. "Did you have fun with jiddo last night?"

"Yes, mama. He told me why I'm not able to see."

"He did?"

There was no frustration in her voice, only light and feathery tones, and Zayan reached out for her, knowing she'd wrap her arms around him tight. He loved the feeling of her warmth; the swell of her pregnant belly. Vanilla and pine and gorgeous hints of lavender from the homemade cream she pasted on her skin after her bath every Saturday.

"What did humans do to get cursed?"

"Well, no one knows for sure, but it was rumoured that humans were destroying the earth. You know how we have farms, and we grow our own food?"

Zayan hummed.

"It wasn't always like that. Before, humans would exploit the lands. They became greedy, growing more food than they needed to; they would poison the soil. There were people starving, and others were obese. They were suffocating mother nature, so it was only fair that she retaliated."

"So people died?"

"People never die, son. Our energy is forever. But their bodies were buried so they could not destroy any more land. Now, only a million people live on the Earth, and they keep it healthy."

Zayan played his mothers words over and over in his head until his baba came home from work that evening, hushed tones and a million kisses on the apple of his cheek as he was thrown over his fathers shoulder. They had a routine. Every evening, his baba would take him to the beach, and tell him how the colours felt as the sun dipped into the soft clouds. They would hike to the highest hill then, and his father would tell him which colours had been engulfed by the darkness and which ones were lagging behind. How the sky felt; how colours felt.

Zayan decided that day that he wanted to go down to the shore. They never went to the shore; Zayan was always afraid. He thought the waves felt much scarier when you couldn't see them. But today, Zayan had this newfound sense of confidence. He wanted to feel the waves pushing and pulling; swaying his body.

When he grabbed his father's hand and pulled him toward the sound of the shore, his baba chuckled and guided him.

"Be careful, son. The waves are harsh when they want to be."

He could not wait to show his younger sister all that he knew. He secretly hoped that he looked like her.

"Baba?"

"Yes, my son?"

They had found a safe spot behind the trees where the wind was just the perfect temperature, blowing strands of his hair on his forehead, brushing and tickling. Baba was sitting on the grass next to him, and he felt his sturdy shoulders against his head.

"How many weeks left?" Zayan whispered.

Zayan knew exactly how many weeks were left, but he was happy for someone else to say it to him. Someone who could see how his mother's belly grew; someone who could see. He often thought about how his little sister would look; if he reached out to touch her small face, would he feel the same curved nose he felt when he touched his own?

"12 weeks, son."

Zayan counted thirteen on his hands and then placed one down. Last week, it was thirteen. His excitement grew and grew until his body could not hold it down. He jumped up, running around his father and keeping his hand on his fathers shoulder.

"Will she be able to see?" he asked later.

"It depends on who will pass. If the person that passes for her can see, she will be able to. But we won't know until she's born."

Zayan thought about the frailty of human life being passed onto another. The thought that anyone could pass at any one moment. The thought created a shudder through him.

"Can you pass?"

"Possibly, but usually, the surge chooses the ones who are ready. Things like sight and hearing and the small things can be transferred, but life is much bigger and much more carefully thought out, and I still have much to do here." His baba spoke, and Zayan knew what he was referring to. His baba worked as a specialist for growing crops, and he brought new kinds of crops everyday, explaining what tasty dishes could be made with them; how they might help prolong life.

"Jiddo told me that the curse can be broken."

"That's nothing but a rumour, son. The curse is a blessing."

"Why?"

"Because if the curse is broken for everyone, life will return to how it was; humans would destroy the Earth. The rumour is that even if the curse is broken, it will only be broken for one person. That means only one person can give sight, speech or the ability to hear. Only one person can give life."

"Only the purest of heart." Zayan said that under his breath so his father could not hear.

In the weeks to come, Zayan formed a tradition with his grandfather. In the night, when the noise and the hum of the generators would travel through the city in a low vibration, using up all the solar energy collected throughout the day, Zayan would climb into his bed and wait patiently for another story. Zayan had an idea of what the story could be every night, but Jiddo would always surprise him with tales of a faraway land where colours felt like chocolate cake.

"I wish I could see what the sky looked like. What yellow looks like." Zayan spoke.

"I wish you could too. But let me tell you how it feels."

Jiddo described how the sky felt when he looked up at the fluffy clouds and how the birds flew in perfect unison. How the sun was too bright to look at, so he couldn't look at it for too long, but the yellow light kissed the Earth too deeply to go unnoticed, and how everything in nature had a sweet melody, connected and ardent. Zayan fell asleep to an image his mind created for him, using Jiddo's words as his guide.

When the time came for his mother to hold his father's hand too tight and wail into the silence, covered in a layer of slick sweat, the sun had already dipped into the night sky.

"Zayan, it's bedtime."

"But--"

"No, we already had this discussion. You will get to hold your sister tomorrow."

Zayan, irritated and solemn, retreated to his room. His jiddo came to tuck him into bed, and held his hands tight. He recited something under his breath, and told Zayan there would be no story tonight.

"Your last story will be tomorrow."

Zayan saw yellow first, but he thought he was dreaming. Then he saw the blue dancing on his bedsheets. His eyes were open, and he saw all the colours burst out at him for the first time. There were soft pinks and soulful whites. Zayan got up slowly, touching his face to see if it was real. He saw his hands for the first time, and ran them over the walls beside his bed. It all made sense now, everything he felt had come alive.

His grandfather had given him sight.

He could never thank his grandfather, because his sister's wails filled the room that morning. He saw a damp trail down his mother's face, and saw her face fall in realisation. She saw him seeing her for the first time.

"Oh my god." mama said, reaching out for him with one arm. He tucked his head into his chest, and gazed down at the baby in her arms.

"I can see her mama. I can see her."

He touched her face, held her in his arms, and saw mama smiling down at him. It was the first time Zayan saw his parents; the way mama always kept her hair on one side, long brown locks falling to her shoulders. His babas hazel eyes, and his long eyelashes. Everything he'd felt was real and feral in front of him.

"Where's jiddo?" he asked after he handed Saria back to mama.

Mama started to cry again, and his baba kneeled down, placing Zayans head into his hands.

"You know how I told you that there's always a life passing for a new one to be born."

Zayan nodded, and his father stayed silent. His father, who was the picture of strength, then started to cry. Tears streamed down his face as he pulled Zayan into his chest.

"Jiddo-- he's gone?"

Baba nodded into the nape of his neck, and Zayan shattered in his arms.

Zayan cried that day more than he's ever cried in his entire life, and he thought it was a cruel irony. The first day of being able to see was tainted by the lack of the only one he wanted to share it with. He wanted to hug Jiddo, and tell him that he loved him. But he could not because Jiddo was gone.

Jiddo was in heaven, where Saria had just come from.

Saria did not open her eyes until two days later. When she did, the doctor told them she was blind. It was expected, of course. But Zayan saw her grandfather's eyes, the same hazel sparks he'd seen in his pictures.

Zayan, over the first few months, taught her how to sit up by herself, holding her tiny back until she did not need him anymore. Saria had her first laugh tasting a strawberry that baba had grown in the backyard. Zayan would reach over and touch her nose while she lay on mama's lap, and he was right. Her nose felt just like his.

On her seventh birthday, Zayan was playing with Saria on the beach, guiding her to the shore. She looked up at him, holding his hand tightly, and looked into his eyes as if she could see him.

It bothered him, and the guilt felt like a thorn in his back, torturing and wounding.

Later, he kissed her forehead as she drifted off to sleep.

"Don't worry, Zayan. Even if everything goes wrong, love will always be there." She whispered, and Zayan's eyes widened in response.

Yellow danced in his eyes the next morning, just like it had every morning since his jiddo kissed his forehead all those years ago. Yellow danced, like it would every morning to come. But something had changed that morning. Because as Zayan gazed at Saria sunk into his chest, he realised that his jiddo was not gone. That his jiddo was living through his little sister. That he was still there with him. In every spec of soil; in every cloud. With his gift, Zayan decided that nobody ever died. Only their bodies would be buried. But they lived on. Through the yellow that danced in his eyes, his jiddo lived on.

3

BREATHE

I never thought about it, not in the way other people had. It never lingered in the depths of my mind for too long. What it meant to be evil. My father never used the word; he forbade it in our cave.

"No one is born evil," he scoffed. "Circumstance makes them evil."

I believed him then, looking up at him with glowy eyes, a mere child looking through a veil of clouded ignorance.

"What about humans?" My brother would challenge him. "Even them?"

And my father would not back down, even for the species that had been hunting our kind for generations, merely due to our trifling differences. Our human faces and our patterned tails. Mainly, they would hunt us for our women.

"Even them," he would say. "Humans are a product of their environment."

I thought my father was wise to provide hope to a world that lacked any. To provide hope to the lingering echoes of fear in our constant moving from one part of the North sea to another. Hope in the chaste kiss on my mother's forehead when she'd stifle her sobs into his chest amid re-packing all our belongings. Hope in the dead bodies of our kind that lay at the bottom of the sea bed, suffocated by a thousand years worth of misery. Hope in our treacherous fight back.

Now though, I feel none.

There's no hope in this dark silent room on the surface where I sleep to the sounds of clattering and shouting from the human bar below. My lips attempt to recreate the sounds of the ocean, but it pales in comparison to the real thing. Hope is the least of my worries here. The worry lives in the frail attempt that my weak, tortured heart is making to beat. In the fragile scars that run across my body echoed by the sounds of human mockery. The worst of it is in the throbbing ache between my thighs. It hurts, even now.

And I can't fight it.

My father had never taught me to fight, he thought it was fruitless to teach a symbol of hope to fight. But my brothers knew better. As more pieces of plastic floated down to the ocean bed and the more fish were found dead on the tops of our cave, the anger built inside my brothers. Rowdy, my father called them.

In the dead of night where the waters were not yet glowy under the sun, they could wake me from my slumber with a shake of my shoulders, and cover my mouth when I tried to shout. I cried copious tears, but obliged when they forced me to aim a rock at them. They would laugh, and mock me, but never stopped teaching me. I bled when their sharpened rocks cut my skin, and my mother would angrily usher me inside the caves while the patience in my father would dampen as he would swim after them to give them a taste of their own medicine.

"Don't worry darling. You only need to fight from here." My mother pointed to my heart, while kissing the wounds that lay on my arm.

And I fought, a little too well.

When the day came to migrate once more, like we would do every few months, the human boat had already found us.

That was the day I became brave, and used my tail to propel myself toward the surface and lead the boat away. I heard their voices in the distance, and I knew they would not see the stinging tears of pain in my eyes, so I never turned back. The real pain came later. The pain that ached my every fibre of being when the metal spikes landed around my tail and pulled me up and out the water.

And now I face the consequences of my decisions, sitting slumped in this dark cold room with nothing but the sound of trees rustling in the wind and the weak chesty sound of my own breath. I am still not used to it, breathing the horrid air that the humans have polluted. Breathing air at all. I wear the shackles around my arms like a prayer and I use the pain to keep my mind focused.

"Pick up a weapon." I hear my brother's voice like he is right next to me. And my eyes shoot open. Another human man stumbles in, already eagerly removing his pants. On land, my body has been reduced to an object, shattering every ounce of hope everytime I think I may escape this hell. It seems distant now; hope is scarce when greed marks the air that humans breathe.

This human is like all the others, the smell of alcohol strong on his breath. I smell it from the other side of the room. He eyes me, his gaze travelling up and down my body in fascination. He smirks, inches closer and pins me below him. He starts kissing my neck and I don't fight it anymore. I'm so tired of fighting it.

The hope comes gradually in the feel of a hardness pressing up against my chest. My eyes shoot down to the blade sticking out of his vest.

Pick up a weapon, I think.

And I hear the words again and again, until I muster up the courage to move my arm from under the human's clutch, and grab the blade.

It's easier than I think, to be evil. And then I think maybe my father was right all along. Maybe circumstance does make us evil.

If evil is his body slumped onto mine, and his staggered breathing and the blood oozing from his chest.

If this is what it means to be evil, then maybe I am evil.

Maybe everyone is.

4

FRENCH TOAST

I felt it in my bones when I left my studio. The cold breeze struck me faster than I could retaliate, and I placed my hands towards my bare neck.

I should have bought that scarf, I think.

I was walking back from work yesterday when the colours jumped out at me. The streets sat in their lonesomeness, dull and grey. In the distance, a few old couples lined up to buy fries, and the outdoor stalls had a plethora of items on sale. Bargaining came at the risk of sounding pretentious, so I decided against it. And I most definitely was not going to pay thirty-five dollars for something as simple as a scarf. My mind couldn't comprehend how that was a sale.

The silky material hung from the hanger, and the colours had a pattern I could lay my eyes on forever. Purple and black and a hint of gold. It almost made me overlook the considerable number on the label above it. Still, my common sense pulled an imaginary clutch, and I headed towards the direction of home, not before the lady at the stall threw me a scowl. She had seen me gaping at the scarf, letting my painted hands hover over the material and widened her eyes at my curiosity. When I turned to leave, aware of her eyes that followed my every move, I became somewhat afraid that the old lady may gather all her strength to chase me away.

Was I not allowed to look?

I had seen the frail older woman several times before, and she had not once smiled back when I attempted to cheer her up. She had a hideous style, her clothes always dull and oversized, and her eyes pierced through me. Like she was always watching.

Something about the day felt bitter, as if the grey clouds were whispering to each other of their own volition. I was a sucker for days like these. Days wrapped up in a coat I wouldn't have to take off, and even if I did, I had prepared myself with a hoodie underneath.

A fifteen-minute bus away, my first class was waiting for me. Communication in art, a course I would surely relish. As I headed toward the bus station, the bench next to it had a peculiarly large amount of leaves hanging on the edge, on the brink of toppling over. I turned my head towards the tree directly above it, shedding leaves and leaving in its wake an enormous mass of colour. My lips tuckered upward as I let my eyes hover over the distinct shades of brown and golden. The textures seemed perfectly dense and warm and intertwined in the most magnificent ways. Most people would think the leaves rotting on the floor were gross and not worth a second look, but I didn't.

They were beautiful in their most refined form, honest and raw, and so flawed they became quintessential—a way for mother nature to be reborn through the seasons. I always thought mother nature was the greatest artist of all time, and every single day, I was proved right.

The entire stage reminded me of a piece of art I had recently cultivated. An article I had never been more proud of, hues of golden brown and green struck with lines and dots and textures I spent hours creating, yet still had not perfected. It was a spontaneous piece inspired by the *Vitruvian man,* symbolising his connectedness to nature. I never particularly liked Da Vinci's work, but that one perplexed me so often I was compelled to work through my doubts through the simple art of, well, art. So that weekend, I was reminded of a small corner shop that sat on the street next to the *lacove museum,* famous for its fragrances and woody feels, that sold acrylic colours. Specific ones I needed for this painting.

And when I took a tram to get there, I was met by the owner who spent two hours explaining to me all the different paints in great detail, starting from their origin to how the truck driver had delivered them late and made him miss his 35th-anniversary dinner. I had reacted calmly, albeit my only focus was to buy the paints I needed and get out of there before he ended up inviting me to explore the artwork in the back, and it was not in my capability to refuse his kind and humble offer. In his eyes sat meek and lowly wisdom, strengthened by the dried paint on his hands that embodied his love for the subject.

When I finally mustered up the courage to say I had to leave, he thanked me for my time and my purchase and placed his hand on his chest. His crooked smile created a maze on his face, wrinkled and tattered and kind. The journey home felt less laborious as the excitement had started to settle in my chest for the piece I would create when I reached home, signified by the constant tapping of my feet against the lined indents on the metal floor.

Two months later, the excitement had dissipated into the winter sky and the unfinished canvas laying on the wood. And now, sitting in art communication, my tired eyes kept giving into the dark, and I had to fight every urge not to let them. I loved this class, but sleep had etched its way into my body and made itself comfortable in the depths of my consciousness, coercing me to step into the dark.

Twenty minutes in, a tall boy pushed the doors open and strolled into the lecture hall. Embarrassment settled on his face in a soft pink colour, and he mumbled an incoherent apology to the teacher before he headed towards the steps. He was carrying a portrait but had it tucked underneath his shoulder, hidden from curious eyes. He took his seat not too far from me, and it compelled me to lean forward to take a peek at the portrait before he placed it flat against the floor. Red hues lined the edges, with a hint of golden brown in tiny dots. But he was quicker than my adjusting eyes, and he had the portrait safely hidden beneath the chair. That only spiked my curiosity further.

After the class ended and most of the crowd huddled through the door, I took my time to pack my laptop in my bag. The boy was still in the front row, typing carefully on his computer, in no hurry to leave.

I have to leave eventually, I thought.

So I gave up and headed towards the front. I didn't quite understand why I was so curious. It was an art school, after all. Everyone had portraits clutched underneath their arms or hidden in their backpacks while walking to class in the morning.

Stopping to open the door, I turned my head back, and he glanced down at me, carefully clutching a paintbrush with another one tucked behind his ear.

And then he smiled. A subtle smile, but it tucked my lips upward. In his eyes was a tantalising calm, and they flickered back to his laptop.

When I had finally reached home, the canvas stood up and stared back at me. Colours screamed at me, and I sighed. It was hard to admit I struggled with it, but I never let the thought settle. Instead, I picked up an art book and tried to trick my stupid brain into being inspired. I plumped myself on the white velvet sofa in the middle of the small room tiled with a beautiful wooden tarnishing, reached out for the thick blanket and splayed it on me, drowning in the comforting feel of warm heaviness.

Before grabbing the art book, I turned to the beautiful portrait that mother nature provided. It was one of my favourite things about this studio—the window.

Outside, I could almost see how cold it was. The fog lingered in the sky, consuming the top of the buildings. But she made up for it. Mother nature had changed the colours of each tree, with beautiful vivid browns, rich yellows and vibrant greens.

My eyes scoured over the artbook my grandfather had given to me as a child. One I had kept in flawless condition. His smile sat in the back of my mind, and I turned towards the portrait I'd drawn of him. An A3 canvas sat on the windowsill, its colours sprouting at the edges and his eyes a sincere brown. The painting was one of my proudest moments, and it brought back the summer I had spent with him, blissful days spent under the sun, where any tension derived from the complexity of our egos washed into the sea. The smell of the sea was ingrained in our skin, effective in reminding us that the view was right outside our window every morning when our refreshed eyes would adjust to the beaming sun. And no matter how many showers we took, they were ineffectual in blurring those memories.

The ache of the absence of my family forced me to get up out of the sofa and into the kitchen, suddenly motivating me to make my mum's famous french toast. I placed the ingredients on the counter and rehearsed my mothers' instructions, her voice bouncing around in my head.

As soon as the first toast was in the pan, a sweet aroma filled the studio, and I revelled in it.

Soon enough, the toast transformed into a beautiful golden brown colour, and I placed a piece in my mouth and closed my eyes as the soft texture grazed my tongue. I made sure to blow on the next piece to avoid burning my tongue. Recalling the last time I had done that with my morning coffee, I spent the rest of the day scowling at the foul taste of every meal I ate. It was a horrible experience.

The fluffy, soft pancakes soothed my intense cravings, the slight hint of vanilla sitting on the tip of my tongue while I typed out my arduous tasks on my laptop for school. I worked my way through all the readings until I came across one that caught my eye.

Body image through strokes in creative art' - Ameliah Larne.

I took my time with it, reading every sentence twice when my eyes would automatically skip over words in a frantic hurry to get to the end. The author had placed examples of symbolism in art on every page, and bare bodies of women of all sizes covered the page. Beauty devoured them whole, and it was the only time I had seen a woman who looked like me and called her beautiful. Curves in all the wrong places and not enough curves in others—covered in spots, perfectly placed with each representing the insecurity behind her brown eyes. And yet, behind her brown eyes was everything but insecurity. It was art. And it was beautiful.

The next day, I was inspired by the patches of grey in the sky, the first sign of the sun in weeks. I reached for a blank canvas and started with yellow strokes, drawing a woman's face in the distance. I outlined it in black and added hints of grey on the edges. The end product looked seraphic, tranquil and composed in a way so transcendent it demanded a smile that sat on my face to my first class.

I trekked along the same street again, and this time the stalls had hidden themselves away inside the stores, afraid of the forecasted rain that would pour down later today. The frail older woman sat inside, and her eyes searched mine before my head turned away. A lack of emotion sat on her face, and she looked menacing.

The thought was shaken off me by a boy in the distance. He had long brown hair tucked underneath his ears and a black coat hanging from his back. He looked tall, taller than he had yesterday, and my legs walked slower in apprehension. Conversing with a younger boy, he placed his arm around him. As the distance between us shortened, I saw the brown eyes of the younger boy. He was smiling, and his smile travelled to his eyes—an identical smile.

Brothers.

I walked past them but couldn't help turning back, hoping the distance would hide my unbridled curiosity. A young woman approached them and spoke in hushed tones, but I was close enough to hear them.

"Go, Eli, before you're late again. I have to get this one to school."

Eli.

She reached for the younger boy's head and pulled him closer to her, running her fingers through his long, brown locks. The boy gleamed at her and wrapped his arms around her tight, placing his head on her stomach. She gave him a small chuckle and turned her head towards Eli again, pointing towards the building I was approaching.

He nodded and high fived the little boy before placing a kiss on the woman's cheek.

"I love you, mama."

By now, I'm pretty sure I looked like an idiot or a lost puppy, so I made sure I got to the school entrance before he noticed me there. But my feet didn't move fast enough.

His languid but lengthy strides caught up to me in no time, and his hand reached for the door before I could.

"After you."

He opened the door, and I looked into his brown eyes before walking in. They twinkled, holding a mischievous cordial look behind beautiful coffee coloured orbs.

"Thank you," I spoke softly, my voice cracking as I placed one foot after another.

How did I forget to walk a mere three minutes after our first interaction?

I internally smacked myself and held the door open for him as he entered. His eyes were trained on me, and behind them, they were searching mine. Like he was looking for something.

His lips turned upward, and I assumed he had found it.

"You're in my communication art class, right?" his voice came out coarse and lower than I expected, and my stomach did a small somersault in return.

We walked in unison, and I managed to nod at him.

"Yes, I took the course at the last minute, but I'm enjoying it so far. How are you finding it?"

His lips once again formed a smile, and it spread to his eyes, leaving me basking in his warm, soothing aura.

It wasn't entirely arcane, but he was magnetising. I immediately wanted to know more about him.

"I quite like it, actually. Mr Ature makes it fun. He makes it feel like we're all in nursery again."

I chuckled slightly but marvelled at his comment. Mr Ature was my favourite teacher. His passion made the classroom feel all the brighter, and he had this beautiful approach to teaching, inspiring and ardent like he wasn't teaching us but learning from us.

"Exactly. He is so inspiring. And did you get a chance to read the articles he assigned to us? I was blown away by the one about body image."

"Yes, I tried to paint the girl in the picture," he said.

"Oh, wow. I'd love to see it."

"Really?"

"Of course."

"I'll be working on it in the art studio after my next class if you want to pass by." He offered.

"Yes, I'd love to."

"Okay, great." He spoke softly and paused before he turned to leave. "I didn't get your name."

"Oh, it's Alora."

"Eli."

I nodded in return and watched curiously as his lips tuckered upward. He turned to walk down the hall, his strides quickening, and he disappeared between the crowds of ecstatic students hurrying in different directions.

It was only then that I realised I was not breathing. His presence was strong, like an invisible piece of thread pulling me closer. I could almost feel him, in a way so unexplainable, I was in trepidation of questioning it.

I forced myself to class, and it dragged on. Of course, it would because all I could think about was after. After -- when I could glance at his daring eyes, and the smirk tugging on his lips and listen to the inspiring nonsense that spoke through him. Like the wind on a hot day. It had drained my patience by the time we were dismissed, and I decided to head to the studio.

I started on a plain new canvas, using my mother's watercolours. My fingers were gentle with soft strokes of pink and black, carving a girl's face with tones of a pretty pink and made her eyes large, hints of bubbly blue and grey-green in her eyes. The project was based on body image, so I outlined a curvy figure inside the orbs—a woman's body sitting in the mirror, free of all identifications. I then drew the mouth of the girl, pulling her lips down slightly. And there it was, the finished piece.

"That's beautiful." His low voice made me jump, and his steps came closer, a deep chesty chuckle forming from within him.

I turned to meet his eyes and drowned in his smile.

"Well, I tried."

"What do you usually think about when you paint?"

"Usually the theme I'm trying to portray."

"Try thinking about nothing."

"What?" I asked, curious.

He lifted a canvas from his bag and set it down onto the easel beside me. It was empty, plain.

"What do you see?"

"What do you mean? There's nothing there."

He cocked his head, and I looked at the painting.

"I see an empty canvas."

He shook his head.

"I see stretched cotton on four pieces of wood."

Again, he shook his head.

"I see potential."

"Correct, but not the answer I'm looking for. Look closer."

So I did. I leaned closer to him and hovered over the canvas.

And there it was, a thin layer of white paint perfectly coated over the canvas.

"Oh."

He smiled at me again.

"When you overthink, you don't see what's right in front of you, even when you're looking right at it."

"So when you paint, you think about nothing?"

"Sometimes, your mind wanders, but the best paintings come when you are present."

Gazing into his eyes once more, the hazel in them sparkled.

"I wanna show you something."

I followed him into the backroom, letting my eyes gaze at the pretty colours that consumed the room. His strides quickened until they halted in front of a finished piece.

My eyes widened at the intricacy of the abstract patterns that devoured the painting, the colours and the tones. It was the same one I had seen clutched under his arm.

"Did you do this?" I stepped closer and let my fingers hover over the canvas.

He nodded his head next to me and leaned in. I breathed a little deeper at the warmth of his body heat.

"The best piece I've probably ever done."

"I.. uh yeah. It's beautiful."

Hesitation sat behind my eyes, but I told the truth. It was beautiful, almost too beautiful.

"When you truly are present when you paint, when that tiny voice dies down, you work through calm, and calm works through you. There are no expectations."

"Expectations?"

"About how it'll turn out. It feels like this."

He then, without stalling, stepped into my space and stood right behind me. I tried to breathe, but it wouldn't work.

"Close your eyes," he whispered in that low voice of his, travelling in murmuring vibrations through me, and I felt his hand on my wrist. And then he was lifting, and I felt the paintbrush softly hit the canvas as his other hand travelled to my waist, barely touching me. I didn't know if it was to keep me balanced or for something else, but I instantly leaned into it.

"Let me work through you."

I nodded, and he carried on.

30

When I eventually opened my eyes after his soft, ushering whispers, the air was clumped at the back of my throat, not being able to find its way to my lungs.

The painting was mostly the same, but it had an element I could not quite pinpoint.

Gorgeous hints of green and hazel coloured the painting, with strokes perfectly aligned with the white below it.

He was still too close to me for me to speak, so I didn't. I let my eyes wander over it again and again until I could find the right words.

"Did you feel it?"

I nodded and instantly missed the heat from his body when he let me go.

Later, we worked side by side. Stolen glances and sips of coffee from his half-filled cappuccino, we painted in tandem. Rhythmic and melodic, through each other.

I finished my piece in record time. And when I stepped back to look at it, Eli did the same. A hand on the small of my back when he whispered into my ear.

"It's ready."

We called it "the moment" and decided it was in my top five.

For weeks after, we would sit in the seats next to each other in class. Often, Eli slipped his hand in mine without realising, fiddling with the ring on my index finger. Nothing had shifted between us, but I learnt more in those weeks than I'd ever learnt.

"Lora, you need to see this," he called for me from the sofa.

After our joint art therapy class, we were in my studio, trying to get the three portraits done for art communication.

I only had "the moment" but desperately wanted to finish the one I had tucked underneath my bed after several failed attempts. I hadn't told Eli about it yet, afraid he would push me to finish it when I knew I wasn't near ready to relive all the chaotic emotions that went into that piece.

"What?" I sat next to him on the sofa, handing him one plate with two slices of french toast.

He gladly took it, handing me his phone in his exchange.

"It's one of her new pieces. They're showing it next week up North."

"Oh my God, it's beautiful. I can't imagine how it's going to look in real life."

Anya was a modern artist our age, and Eli and I agreed we would die for her paintings.

"We should go."

I pulled up my timetable.

"We have two classes that day."

"Two classes we can skip for our dear friend, Anya."

"Eli." I tried to stay stern, but the mischievous glint in his eyes told me he was not letting this one go.

"Lulu." he almost whined, and I went to smack his chest.

"Stop calling me that. Fine, we'll see."

"We can skip one class. Mr Ature will understand."

He made this sad face, his lips turning peculiarly towards his chin.

"Puppy eyes don't suit you. Shut up and eat your french toast before it gets cold."

The week flew by, and on Tuesday night after our evening class, Eli pulled me into a vacant room and shoved two tickets in my face, leaning closer than he needed to.

"Wear something nice."

He left then, a smile tugging at my lips and a brimming of feelings growing like a storm in the centre of my stomach.

And Tuesday came quickly, along with the first signs of Spring. Pink cherry blossoms had made themselves known on the trees outside my studio window. Standing tall and gently swaying with the wind, the pink gleamed gorgeously in the rays of the sun.

I had worked the whole day, watching my breath as Eli had taught me and scrapping my expectations and now, sitting in front of me was my second finished piece. It was an onion in the shape of an eye, layers peeling off the sides. My fingers were tainted with many colours from my palette, and I had no time to wash them off.

The weather was humid today, a heat wave winding through the small town, so a dark brown satin dress was the only dress in my cupboard that jumped at me.

I had never worn it, my body an uncomfortable collection of wrong turns and curves I wanted to cover. I found myself trembling as I pulled the satin over my head.

It sat on my body rather oddly, but because I knew Eli wouldn't think twice about all the several things I was insecure about and there was no time to hunt for something new, I found the confidence to keep it on.

"You do know we're going to be late."

Eli had come to pick me up, prepared with a bottle of wine and two glasses. The boy was absurdly eager to have a drink before leaving because it was 'classy'. I rolled my eyes, and he chuckled.

"Don't rush a lady Eli," I called from where I was seated in front of my lengthy mirror, hidden from his curious eyes.

"You probably look gorgeous. Please come out."

"Coming."

And I did, red-stained on my lips and concealer under my eyes. I gulped, his eyes first landing on my face. I was glad there was no glass in his hand because his arms fell limp as soon as his mouth slightly fell.

After exploring every inch of my body, he finally breathed when his eyes reached mine again.

"What?" I asked, my lips pursed.

"You- you're art."

He came closer then, reaching for me. His hands found my neck, and he pulled me up, so his lips barely grazed my forehead. Shivers slithered through me and my heart trembled inside my chest.

He then took my hand, led me to the table, handed me a glass of wine, and we clinked them, sounds of combined laughter echoed through my studio afterwards.

We left soon after, finding ourselves holding each other on the train there. His arm wrapped around my waist as he whispered in my ear all the things he was excited about. I agreed to every one of his long lists, mumbling into his chest. I took it all in, his woody musky perfume and the feel of his body against mine. The way his fingers would catch onto the strings of satin on my bare back, and he'd twist them around his finger. His breath against my neck and his voice. Low and lulling.

The art was as beautiful as we both imagined, and we were both in awe through every piece of work we saw. The entire gallery was a piece of heaven on Earth, bursting with colour.

I stood, lonesome, next to the modern painting called 'hell' with lines of gold and black winding through the canvas. Eli was on the other end of the gallery, attempting to figure out what colour the artist used in one of the modern art paintings, his phone clutched tightly in his hand as he carried out several google searches.

I smiled at his absurdity.

"A true artist always has paint on her body." a voice came from behind me.

I recognised it instantly.

I smiled shyly, chuckled and looked down at my fingers, shades of bubbly blue and pretty pink all over them.

"I had no time to wash them off."

She was gorgeous, with hazel eyes and dark olive skin. Seeing her in pictures online did not compare.

"So, what do you think?" she gazed away from me.

"I think-- there's so much truth in it, but you're deceiving yourself."

"Excuse me?"

"You make hell look beautiful, but it's not, is it?"

I could see her lips turn upward, and it radiated through me.

"Hell is beautiful when you've walked through it and look back at it from a distance." she said.

Shivers prickled at my skin like thorns on a rose.

"What do you lean toward when you paint?"

"Well, I'm still in school, so I paint based on what I'm assigned."

"That wasn't my question."

Her words made me smile. "I like painting my insecurities, but recently I've been letting it paint through me."

"That sounds intriguing, do tell."

So I did. We conversed for several minutes before Eli approached us with his giddy eyes and a flickering shy gaze.

Eli told Anya about all his favourite pieces of hers, and when Anya asked why, he said that it didn't feel like a human made it. She had chuckled at that.

A tall man approached us, arcane with dark eyes, jet black hair, and an upright stance. I had to strain my neck to look at him.

"I want you guys to meet someone. This is Marco, and he's the owner of the studio and several others. He made this all happen." Anya spoke, a loving melody in her voice as she reached for him.

He didn't seem like the type I thought she would have, but then he smiled and reached for the small of her back, and it was nothing but love between the two.

Afterwards, when we had talked about every art piece there was to talk about, me and Eli had gone outside by the terrace. When Eli grabbed my hand and whispered, "I want to show you something", it surprised me. I put the small piece of paper with Marco's phone number inside my bag and let his hand take me into the dark.

The night was quiet, and the wind was whispering to the trees, playing hide and seek under the moonlight. Yellow hues dispersed from the lights on the bridge, and Eli kept going.

Only when I was breathless did he finally stop.

"We're here."

My head searched for something out of the ordinary, but all I saw was the dock, deader than the night.

Before I had a chance to speak, there it was. A boat, large and lively with chatter, approached us.

And then he gleamed at me and gave me his most mischievous grin yet.

"We're going on that?"

"Well--"

"What?"

"We're sneaking on that."

"What-- Eli, no."

"Yes."

We did, and not at my accord. The boat came closer, and he jumped first, landing by the jet skis. And then he reached for me, my heart pounding in my chest and my legs trembling, my eyes trained on him.

He was my only destination.

Five minutes in, we had found a spot by the pretty pink flowers, Eli pressed his body up against mine. He took his time, gazing at every inch of my face and his hands slyly positioned at my waist. And when his hand shifted to the sensitive space on my back, his face inched closer.

Our lips met, soft and gentle. And then Eli was moving in search of me, and we were sharing the same air. Soon, it turned desperate, and his hands were all over me, burning every inch of skin, sending a pleasant rush of life through my bones. I reached for him, holding him so close to my body, I wasn't sure who was who.

When we finally pushed away, out of breath but holding each other as nothing would ever be enough, we both silently agreed to go home.

The next few weeks, I woke up leaning into him, the heat from his very body placed behind me coercing me to reach for him. And I did. Sometimes, I'd find him in my kitchen, trying to perfect his french toast. I'd be in awe but stay angry until his lips found mine, and his arms lifted me onto the kitchen counter, laughing as he breathed into my neck, tickling the skin with his barely-there beard.

The first time he said I love you was by mistake, our bodies collided in the summer heat after dinner on the pier. I had stolen his shirt, and I refused to give it back. So he chased me, unwilling to give up. Pinning my body onto the bed, he whispered them into my ear.

I stared into him and let each of my fingers glide over every crevice on his face, finding the back of his neck and pulling him toward me.

"I love you."

It was only in September when the trees were once again shedding their leaves to keep the earth warm for winter, did I find the piece of art that lay unfinished and abandoned under my bed. Eli had flown to Italy for the semester, and his dip on my bed was fading.

I craved his presence dearly, but the canvas kept me busy. I had started with shades of brown and then dots of black around the jaw of the woman's face and had breathed through every step. I dreamt of how it might turn out, but every morning I forgot what the dreams told me, and I was left with nothing but the air in my lungs and the passing thoughts in my mind.

I ignored each of his calls when I painted, and soon he got impatient.

"How important could this piece be?"

"If you came back, you would see."

"Baby, you know how much I want to."

"I know."

He did eventually, but the piece was not finished yet. I picked him up from the airport and reached for him as if we'd been away for years. My heart ached for his scent, and the moment his body was on mine, I bathed in it.

Only when I was satiated from the hunger of him did he ask me about the piece, but I refused to show him. And he asked again, and I shook my head. But the boy was anything but patient and kept asking me every day for the next week.

"Eli, I can't show you until it's done."

"Why? You've always shown me your unfinished pieces."

"It's all my-- it's everything I'm afraid of."

My voice came out shaky, and it made him grip my hand a little tighter.

"Then I'll wait, but only if you promise to show me when you're ready."

"I will."

He did a fine job of waiting because the last stroke came to me in the dead of night, and I jumped up and out of bed, causing him to jump up in fright.

I kissed his forehead, apologised and ran to the other room.

It looked magnificent as the sun rose, the rays hitting the piece perfectly. The colours shone, danced, and took their time to come together.

It was the best piece I'd ever done, and I knew Eli agreed when I called him from the other room after making him wait for four hours, he strolled in, shirtless and giddy. When he saw it, his mouth hung open. He stayed silent for minutes after, touching the piece over and over again, like he'd never seen colours before.

The piece was an outline of a female face, every colour spreading through and out towards the end. There was an outline of a body in her eye and birds flying from her mouth.

"It looks like heaven and hell, in the same piece."

My lips tugged at his words.

He recognised the other eye, I could tell, but didn't say anything until he stared at it.

"Is that- my eye?"

I nodded when he finally faced me.

"I love the way you look at me. I never want you to stop."

A single tear rolled down his cheek, and he nibbled at the insides of his lips.

And then he reached for me and hugged me so tight. I could almost feel our bones merging as one.

Eli bugged me to call Marco, but I refused. I knew he would do it if I didn't, so I wasn't surprised when I heard his whispers from the other room.

I trembled as I uncovered it, placing the canvas on the easel in Marco's gallery, and Eli slipped his hand in mine.

The silence was the only praise I received from them, and it was the only one I needed.

"Am I allowed to say that this is better than most pieces I've seen, or would you kill me?" Marco spoke.

"I would not kill you because you're not wrong." Anya chuckled, running her fingers over the paint.

Marco agreed to display it, and it saddened me to hand it away, but I had memorised every colour and stroke, so I would never forget.

And it was a Monday in mid-November when I received the call about the potential buyer, and my heart beat fiercely against my chest.

I took days, drowning in the sofa with the weight of Eli's body wrapped against my abdomen, to decide, but eventually agreed to sell it. We had to give it a name, so me and Eli decided on 'French Toast'.

Marco had sold it for thousands of dollars and gave me eighty per cent, along with a contract to keep showing my work.

"Five pieces. After that, I'll gladly give you a room." He spoke, excitement lining his voice. After that, we all became friends, sharing dinners and drinks over conversations about modern art.

It was sad to see the piece leave with no idea of its destination, but the buyer wanted to stay anonymous. So I let it go, keeping a replica that Eli and I had spent all night making as the main attraction in my studio.

For weeks after, I longed to see the painting. I sat in my bed after being woken up by Eli and his heavy hand around my waist and closed my eyes tightly shut, waiting for it to pop up. But it never did.

Soon, the winds turned biting cold, and my neck only felt warmth when Eli wrapped his arms around me, placing his mouth all over.

It was a Wednesday on the streets when my eyes caught sight of something familiar, and my stomach dropped onto the cold hard pavement. There it was, French Toast, in all its glory. Tucked in the corner shop, guarded by an old lady. I didn't blink until I approached it, hidden behind the piles of clothes in the corner.

"It's not for sale." she croaked, old and frail.

"It's lovely."

"It's not for sale." She said again, slightly louder this time. When my eyes reached hers, I saw the colours radiating from her clothes, and my lips turned upward.

"Is this?" I picked up the scarf that lay hanging on the rack. The same one I had marvelled at a year ago.

The older woman nodded fiercely.

"How much?"

"What's your name?"

"Alora."

"Fifty dollars."

And I knew that she was overcharging me ridiculously, but I handed her the note anyway, and she snatched it from my hand.

"Alora," she spoke in an almost whisper as I turned to leave, the scarf carefully tucked beneath my arm.

A smile played at her lips. "It is lovely." And then she nodded and pointed to the painting like she knew it was mine.

Turning her body away from me, I watched as she tucked the note inside a jar.

When I left the warmth, the biting cold returned, prickling the nape of my neck.

Eli was waiting for me outside, a gleam plastered on his face. When his eyes landed on the scarf on my arm, he reached for it. Wrapping it around my neck, he pulled me closer. His lips went in search of mine, and a chuckle escaped me. My hands found the dips in his chest and he kissed my forehead.

"I like the scarf, darling."

"Me too."

And winter was back. The cold whistling of the wind travelled through the streets of the small town, and my painting was safe, tucked in the corner of a street shop.

Winter didn't feel so terrifying anymore, with a hand wrapped in mine and a warm scarf on my neck and an empty canvas waiting for me when I got home.

5

DELUDE

The stone reaches out to him, screaming and urging for him to pick it up. Bari does, and his fingers run over the inscription that his father had carved out when he was a boy, peeking behind the half-closed door of their large beige living room, trying to stay hidden in the shadows. His father knew he was there, and ushered for him, reaching out his hand and pulling him close against his chest. Bari felt the slow beating of his heart, and wondered why his heartbeat was dissimilar. His heartbeat was as fierce as the rain on the window on a stormy day.

His father kneeled, slipping the stone inside his shaky hand, and whispered something in his ear.

"Some things are worth fighting for."

His lips mouth the words now. The stone is the only thing he had kept over the years, the only constant. The stone is a stone, and that's all it will ever be. It has no ulterior motive. Bari can't say the same about everything else in his life.

The clamour of the ship roars, and he is summoned by his co-pilot, Kamail. Bari puts the stone back into the box and walks out of his chambers, into the flight deck. He peers to the controls, nodding to Chari. Her almond eyes glimmer under the yellow lights. She tucks her lengthy dreads to one side and clicks a few buttons on her tablet, popping the route and the mission details on a hologram. Bari steps back to analyse it.

"We seem to be on course. What's our ETA?"

Chari points to the right end of the hologram, where a few numbers wobble as the ship moves.

"How bad at maths do you think I am?"

Chari shrugs, humour painting her eyes. "It's fun to watch you struggle."

He scoffs, leaning into the hologram and makes a few small calculations in his head. "Two days."

The two start to clap behind him, and Bari rolls his eyes as they chuckle. He'll give it to them; Bari knows this repose won't last long. As he glances at his team, Kamail squeezing Charis shoulder and leaning to kiss her cheek, he hopes this mission is the last one.

Chari flings her tablet toward him and says *look*.

Big brown almond eyes stare back at him, and his heart swells. Tina's coils have started to grow a few inches and her cheeks look chubbier. She smiles at the camera, her eyes damp like the day she was born when Bari had stumbled through the corridors with wilting flowers he had picked out in a rush. He had been so nervous that day, to see the baby they'd been eagerly waiting for. Of all the things Bari knew about Kamail, he'd always wanted to be a father.

As if by cruel frolicking, Tina was born a spitting image of her mother.

"Are you sure you're the father?"

Kamail flips him off, and the two of them share a look. "I'm not complaining."

Amidst their smile, Bari knows they miss her, and his heart sinks a little. He hands the tablet back to Chari and goes to check on the defence systems downstairs.

He doesn't even make it past the door.

He freezes, the pain slithering around his body and into splitting waves of pain on the right of his chest. He gasps, clutching his chest and his eyes squeeze shut. He holds onto the door with one hand, trying to balance himself until his knuckles turn white. He hopes it passes before they notice, but an arm wraps around his waist, and Kamail holds him upright.

"Woah, breathe." Kamail says, but Bari hears him like he's miles away because the pain rings in his ears, constricting his chest and he slips. Chari grabs his other side as they position him on a chair.

"They're hurting her." He gasps. "They're hurting her."

"Okay, okay." Chari puts her hand on his chest. "Focus on the way my hand feels against your chest. Just like yesterday. Come on, Bari."

The pain lingers, little prickles in and around his chest but he can breathe again. He's still gasping when Kamail sticks the patch on his inner forearm. "Your anxiety makes it worse. Bari, why don't you just take the pills?"

"You know why." Bari says.

"Bari, this much pain can be bad for the link. You can risk going mad."

"I don't care."

They share a look. He knows what they think. Why does he feel her pain when he has the chance to eradicate it? Why does he insist on fighting for her when the chances of finding her are slim to none?

But they do know because they keep quiet. Chari leans against his shoulder. "Just don't die on us."

He won't, but he may well come close.

The patch soothes his nerves, and he positions his head back onto the chair. "I won't."

In fuzzy waves, his memory seeps into the day this all started.

Then

Bari walks slowly enough for his mother to place a gentle hand on his back, urging him forward. The platform where he stands, usually vibrant with colour and intricate patterns, feels duller today. Zerumas sky is rolling with clouds. The cheery crowds are on either side of him, chattering quietly among themselves as he walks across the white stone platform decorated with rose petals.

When the music starts, his breath gets stuck in his throat. His face is hot, burning and his heart races. The necklace on his chest vibrates. A prickle lands on his arm, the needle jabbing him twice. He's instantly calmer.

"Head up." His mum says, and Bari's eyes flicker around and land on the back of his fathers head. His father stands tall, chin up like he's proud of his first born as his duty as leader of the colony compels him to be. Inside, Bari knows he's churning.

This morning, Bari stood in front of his mirror, glancing at his tired eyes and heard the bickering coming from the other room.

"This is not right." His mother said to his father in a low voice. "He is too young, and he doesn't love her."

"What would you have me do instead, my love?"

She had stayed quiet. "I don't know."

Bari heard her muffled sobs through the thin walls and had stopped listening, afraid he would cry too.

Later when he had gone to take a raisin bread roll from the kitchen, she had swollen eyes.

"You're not supposed to eat before the link, Jabari." She said sternly.

He went to put it back.

"But I won't tell anyone." She smiled. His heart sank, knowing what was to come.

Behind every one of his fathers decision, she had been there to question him. Behind everyone one of his decisions, was hers.

Bari knew this was the only one left.

His feet land on the white carpets, at the entrance of the palace. His breath falters, and his eyes fall to his bride. She stares right back at him, her eyes dark with something he can't place. Bari has seen her once before, on the training field. He had woken to the sounds of chaos, and people in the city were talking about a marriage arrangement.

Naturally, Bari had been curious and went to the field to look at the bride-to-be, ignorant to the whispers about the mystery husband being about him. He saw her scar first, starting from her neck and travelling down her arm, ending right next to her pinky. She did not smile when she saw him, instead she looked away.

"Please step forward, Jabari, son of Ayi."

"Aliyah, daughter of Zulki, please rise."

She stands opposite him, her brown eyes wide and her face void of any emotion, and Bari hates her, and it dawns on him he can't for long.

"Link."

Bari puts out his palms, and she peers at them before placing her hands in his. Her jaw is clenched, and a queasy storm stirs at the base of his throat because everything about her screams indifference.

The priest makes the cut on his inner forearm with a silver knife. He does the same with her and then from the box, he removes the link.

Bari has never seen it this close. He pulls the two parts away from each other, and the strings, which look like octopus legs, flail around.

"Jabari, son of Ayi, do you vow to not violate the laws of linking?"

Bari nods.

"Do you vow to respect the link with Aliyah, daughter of Zulki?"

Does he? Will he be okay with her lingering around in his mind? He nods.

"Lastly, are you ready to be linked?"

No, he's not. He nods.

As soon as it's inside his forearm, he squints and tries to maintain his composure as the strings attach themselves to his veins. He feels four prickles and the pain stops.

The priest places the other half of the linker in her arm, and her face remains cold and emotionless as the skin in her forearm settles.

Bari walks a little closer to her and grabs her hands.

As tradition demands, he closes his eyes and places his lips on hers. It's a soft, gentle kiss and they both pull away at the same time.

"Link." The priest says, and Aliyah raises her forearm. Bari does the same and entangles their fingers together. The strings come out of both of their arms and entwine. She buries her head in his chest when the pain comes, and her body feels fragile against him. Somehow, the gesture calms Bari.

Closing in like a fog, he feels her in his mind. It's an unfamiliar sensation, and it's the first time he looks at her and truly sees her. Her favourite colour is gold, like the gold tablecloth her grandma used when she was a child. She likes to imagine how Earth would look like now. She gets along with her father more than her mother. Her heart belongs to another.

They stare at each other for a while, silently memorising every fact about each other. Bari breaks eye contact first.

They make their way out of the palace, hand in hand. His father walks behind them, and the crowds applause and cheer. They celebrate the peace this link will bring. The end of what would've been the greatest war in history between the colonies. Bari's marriage to Aliyah is merely the beginning.

Later, when they have settled in the house, unpacking their things in separate rooms, Bari receives a visit from his doctor.

"You can't have the injections anymore, Bari." His doctor sits opposite him, leaning forward.

"What?"

"We can't risk interfering with the technology. It's very sensitive. I've got my best student working on coding, but you'll have to live with your anxiety for now."

Aliyah's behind the door, he feels her. She hears them, but she doesn't mean to. He feels the dry of her mouth in his.

"Sensitive how?"

"Everything. One mistake, you'll risk delusions. You might hear or see things based on memories or emotions."

He closes his eyes. "How long will it take?"

"Kamail is good, but he won't be done until it's perfect. You're going to have to find another way to cope."

Bari nods okay and leads the doctor to the door. He watches as the doctor walks on the steps, taking with him the necklace in a closed fist. He wants to cry.

Instead, he walks to the kitchen and fills a glass of water. His bare feet pad against the carpeted stairs and enters her room, the door slightly open. The room is dark, moonlight dancing on the bed sheets where he sees a dark figure. He leaves the glass on her bedside table.

For a moment, he thinks maybe she's asleep. He turns to leave.

"I'm sorry." She whispers in the dark.

He releases the breath he didn't know he'd been holding.

As he sinks into his bed, he pulls the quilt to his chest. Bari lays awake for so long, he loses track of time. When he finally falls asleep, it's her bronze skin he sees first. It's her scar against his mouth and her long locks between his fingers. She lays under him, her eyes dark, holding all the secrets he now has access to. It's all of her, all at once.

Now

Sounds of alarms ring through his ears, and he jumps out of his covers. Shirtless, he runs to the front deck.

"God, I was hoping you were still knocked out." Kamail says, moving around the hologram and zooming into the red warning sign.

Chari throws him a shirt.

"What is it?" Bari says as he pulls the shirt over his head.

"It's a warning. The coding on this defence system is extravagant."

"Coming from the guy who coded it." Bari says.

The red starts to spread.

"Delta is attacking the planet."

"Now?"

Kamail nods.

"Shit."

"I need your commands." Chari says, her eyes wide and her hands on the controls.

Bari thinks, and squeezes his eyes shut. What would Aliyah do?

"Turn her around."

"What?" Kamail says, his eyebrows folding.

"You heard me. I won't risk it."

"Bari, if we turn around now, it'll be a months reroute. If she's on this planet, this is our chance."

"And if we get killed in the process, then what? Your baby is waiting for you at home, I'm not risking leaving her an orphan. Get out of here, I'm not saying it again."

Chari goes for the controls, but Kamail stops her with a touch on her shoulder.

"You feel so much of her pain. How long do you think you can keep that up? How long till you wither away Bari? I've told you so many times to take the pills, and you refuse because you're so adamant on finding her, on feeling her. And now, we've finally got a clue and we're turning away?"

Bari rethinks. He looks to Chari, who's solemnly nodding. "He's right, Bari. We've looked everywhere else. I need her back too."

Bari nods, whispers okay and awaits their landing, his hands trembling under the table.

They get there, landing with no imminent signs of danger. They find a sandy terrain, and land far enough to go undetected. Bari hears it though, they all do. Sounds of war. Sounds of pain. Silently, they help each other get ready. None of them mention the fear, but it lingers in the air.

Kamail hands them a circular metal button.

"I coded some new armour technology."

Pressing the button against his chest, the armour slithers atop his skin.

"Lazerproof?"

Kamail grimaces. "That was a 2100 thing. Keep up, Bari."

"Oh, sorry big boy." Bari raises his hand in surrender, his lips turning upward.

Kamail smacks him over the head.

"Boys, stop fighting and save it for the damn pirates."

"Way to spoil the fun." Kamail walks to Chari and plants a kiss on her forehead. "But since I'm actually afraid of you--" he leans down to kiss her lips.

Chari scowls, and Kamail runs out of the room. A sad smile lingers on Chari.

"Nothing will happen to either of you."

Her almond eyes glisten. When she stays quiet, Bari reaches for her hand. "I promise."

"You know when I met you, I thought you were an asshole."

Bari can't help but laugh. "I'd like to say that's because you only had eyes for Kamail."

She shrugs. "I thought you wouldn't be enough for Aliyah."

"Have I proved myself?"

"More than. You fight for her like no one else has. She's my best friend, and that's why I came on this ship when you asked me to. But now, today, I'm fighting for you."

Bari only feels the dampness on his cheek when he pulls her into a hug and she brushes his tears off with the pad of her thumb.

"I will protect you with my life." He whispers into the top of her braids. He feels the love like layers. It doesn't belong to him though. It belongs to Aliyah.

They know what to look for. They know what to avoid. Hiding between rocks and old ship wreckage, they make their way through the sandy terrain, crouching when they hear any sound of danger.

Its not the time to fight, it's the time to hide. Hide from anything keeping him away from her.

"What planet is this?" Chari whispers looking over the rocks to the flaming city in the distance.

Kamail shrugs. "I couldn't find its name anywhere, but my satellites caught the Delta here."

"What's there to pirate here? It looks like a wasteland."

Bari doesn't say anything, but his skin prickles with heat. He looks to the flames in the distance. She has to be here.

"Let's go." Bari says and moves behind the next rock.

Before they can move, Bari hears a gunshot. They duck, and he sees Chari's wide eyes.

"Or not." Kamail moves closer to them.

"Check the activity."

Kamail looks at his tablet. "Shit."

"What?"

"They're close."

"How close?"

"124 metres."

Bari wants to swear. "Let's go."

"Are you crazy?" Kamail says.

"If they find us, we're dead. Look around us, we're trapped. If we go now, we have a chance."

"Bari, what's your plan? Do you even have one?" Chari says.

"First, we get out of here. Then, when we're not surrounded, we can figure it out."

They crouch behind the rocks, moving behind one and then another. Sand scrapes between his toes. The abandoned building seems like a good enough place to hide out, but it's fifty metres of a battlezone, and with a small turn of a head, a sniper would get them. Bari calculates if it's worth it.

He doesn't get to make the decision before Kamail starts to run.

"Shit, Kamail."

He nods at Chari, grabs her hand and they both run, swimming in a sea of sand.

It happens in slow motion, a flash in his eyes and a pained ringing in his ears. Sand flies around him, and the air knocks out of his lungs. He gasps on the ground, trying to regain his composure.

His eyes fall to the rocks at his side, identical to his. *Earth*. He gasps, and looks to Chari.

His heart drops.

She stands, her hand clutching her lower abdomen, blood staining her clothes, spreading like a virus. Chari's lower lip trembles, and he wants to move toward her. He attempts to grab something to help him, but only sand runs through his fingers, and his body slumps back to the ground. Tears burn as they run down his cheeks.

When she falls, everything goes black.

Then

Weeks pass, but with each day, Aliyah etches into his mind. They don't say much, but Bari finds his mug filled with coffee in the morning, with a dash of milk. She doesn't drink coffee.

Bari folds the blanket on the sofa after she goes upstairs because she always forgets. On the days she's awake with her head buried in a book, she always stops outside his door and whispers goodnight. Usually, he doesn't hear her. Today, his eyes blinking in the dark, he does.

"Wait." Bari says.

She opens the door slightly, and her eyes stare into his. He reaches for his side drawer, pulls out a blue box and extends his arm out to her.

"I don't like gifts." She says coldly.

"It's not for you."

She takes it, opens it and her eyes grow wide.

"Is this from Earth?"

He nods.

"It helps me sleep."

"How did you get it?"

"My father. From his. When they were leaving Earth, my grandad went back out in the polluted air at the last minute and came back with this stone in his hand. When my father gave it to me, he told me something."

"What?"

"Some things are worth fighting for."

Aliyah stared at him, and then back to the stone.

"I know this arrangement seems archaic. I know it's fraught. But I just remind myself we're fighting for something. For our people."

"My people were perfectly fine."

"An agreement with the delta colonies is what you call fine?"

Through the small light peeking through his window, Aliyah's jaw clenches and her voice goes low. "No, but at least I had my freedom."

Bari knows, so he doesn't say anything.

"When the Delta started to pirate, the only choice we had was to join colonies. Before this, I was free to fight and go out and live my life. But this link. It's horrible, and it makes me feel cramped. It exposes me to someone I barely know. And for what? Just to make sure your colony doesn't betray mine?" She stops to breathe and a tear threatens to fall from her eye. In a whisper, she says "Isn't marriage supposed to be about love?"

Bari drops his head. He doesn't have anything to say.

"I'm sorry, I'll go."

"No wait." He reaches out for her. He asks her to come with him to the ring tomorrow, to fight.

Aliyah ponders and then nods.

"I never wanted this either." He says.

"I know." She heads toward the door.

"Take the stone."

She shakes her head. "You keep it, everything you feel, I feel."

The first thing Bari feels is his lungs closing in on him. Then, he sees Aliyah in a flash, almost dreamlike, lying on a bed. He sees a man, her hand on his face. Bodies intertwined. He hears her, softly breathing. Bari tries to shake it off, but it persists. He's lost in her memory, fumbling around until he finds something to latch onto.

He goes to run his hand over the pale line of skin around his neck, and he feels her hands instead.

"Go away." He whispers. She doesn't.

"Breathe with me, Bari."

His heart races, and he can't move. His limbs are glued to the bed.

"Bari. Wake up."

His eyes blink open and he sees Aliyah crouching beside him.

"Woah, breathe."

He jerks up, panting.

"It was just a dream."

"No," he puts his hand on his chest. "It wasn't."

"What?"

"I was in your mind. I was stuck."

"What do you mean?"

"I mean, I saw you. In your memories. I couldn't get out."

"How is that possible?"

Bari shrugs. "The doctor mentioned delusions if we messed with the technology. But I'm assuming this memory was real, so I guess it's one of the side effects."

"What did you see?"

The words lodge in his throat. He pictures it and looks at her. She knows.

"Oh." Her face falls. "I'm sorry."

"Don't be."

There's a beat of silence. He thinks maybe she feels uncomfortable, but then she sits next to him on the bed, her eyes shining in the moonlight. He taps lightly, and she gets under the covers. They don't speak, but Bari doesn't remember falling asleep.

When the morning sun gapes through the windows, Aliyah's body is tangled in his. They must have drifted toward each other in the night. He wraps his fingers around her waist and pulls her closer as she stirs against him, her palm landing flat against his chest.

Instead of speeding up, his heart slows.

Now

The overwhelming pain spreads across his body. Sounds of sobbing echo in his head. He jerks awake.

It's dark, the only light shines from the headlight on Kamails headband. It casts a shadow over his face, scarred and bloody. Tears fall off the edge of his nose. He has his hand in Charis, kneeling over her.

"What happened? Is she--?"

"Barely." Kamail sniffs. "After they left, I dragged you two here. Bari she-- she hasn't woken up yet."

Bari moves closer to Chari, wincing as the pain travels through his body. Her body is still. She rasps, her eyes closed and her mouth slightly ajar.

"I removed the shards and cauterised her wound. She was awake when I-- she talked me through it, but then she fell asleep, and she isn't awake yet. Bari, why isn't she awake?"

Bari's tears fall on the sand, and he moves the braids from Chari's face. "Okay, okay. How are her vitals?"

"Fine, everything's fine." Kamail weeps and rests his head against her chest. "Please baby wake up." He whispers.

"We need to get her out of here."

"Bari, we're surrounded. There's no way we're leaving alive."

"So what? We wait?"

"No, we call for help."

"Kamail, no. The signal will be heard by every colony."

"I don't care."

"Kamail."

"We don't have a choice." He cries, his eyes bloodshot when he looks at him. "Bari, she doesn't have time."

He goes for the radio, and Bari doesn't fight him. She won't survive if he doesn't.

So Kamail calls for help and grips the radio harder than he needs to. Both of them tremble in the dark, hoping someone will find them before the soldiers do.

His eyes shut and he calls for her, hoping she hears him. He couldn't save her, but maybe she'll save them.

He's right.

Bari hears her voice. "Bari, wake up."

"Aliyah?" his eyes blink open. He sees the blurry outline of her face.

"Bari get up, you have to leave."

"What?"

He looks to Kamail, who's carrying Chari. His sad eyes stare back at him from a distance.

Aliyah crouches beside him, two soldiers behind her, hands on their guns.

"You're here." Bari goes to touch her cheek. She stops him, her eyes dark.

"Take them to the ship, protect them." Aliyah gestures to the guards. They head to the door and Kamail glances back at him in regret.

Bari looks at Aliyah, and he can't feel her anymore. He doesn't feel her lingering around his mind anymore, and he can barely recognise the look on her face.

"What's going on?"

Aliyah doesn't flinch. He can't read her.

"Why can't I feel you anymore?" He pushes himself off the floor.

"Because I undid it."

"You what?" Tears burn his eyes, but he doesn't let them fall.

"Bari, I can't explain. You have to go."

"No, I came for you. I'm not leaving without you."

"Bari, I'm not coming with you." Aliyah is cold, her face void of emotion. "They'll kill you; Delta will kill you. Get Chari home, now."

"What about us?"

"There is no us. I would say I'm sorry Bari, but I'm not. I never loved you."

He shakes his head, and the tears fall. "You're lying. I felt it."

"Bari, go home. Go home before they shoot you."

He wants to cry, fall, and melt into the sand below him, but he holds his weight and looks her in the eye. "Just tell me why."

She breathes out, her eyes flicker. "I lured you here because it was the only way I could unlink us. We had to be in close proximity."

He nods. "Okay."

He bends, grabs his bag, and walks past her. His skin burns, his breath catching in his throat.

"I am sorry it had to come to this Bari."

He doesn't look back.

He waits till the evening when he's in his room on the ship heading home to muffle his cries into his sheets, hoping they don't hear him.

Then

Bari finds her mouth on his, waking him from his slumber. She kisses him again, pushing her body closer and he reacts instantly, wrapping his hand around her waist and pulling her atop of him. Her mouth feels familiar, moving against him like she knows everything he likes.

54

She muffles her desire in quiet gasps into his. He feels it all, every happy moment gracefully lingering in his head. His anxiety ruffles, never quite making it to the base of his heart. It knows to stay away when she's with him.

As the sun blazes in the horizon, Bari waits for Aliyah to come home. His fingers tighten around his cup, looking over the city he calls home. For the first time, he feels nothing but the smile lingering at the edge of his lips. He never wanted her, but now he has her, he wouldn't want it any other way.

He doesn't hear the click of the door until the early morning. He rushes to the door, his breath heavy and panicked.

He jerks when his father looks at him hesitantly, pain flickering in his eyes.

His heart drops.

"Bari, it's Aliyah."

Now

Maybe he never had her.

For two weeks after they return to Zeruma, Bari doesn't leave his room. He receives visits from Kamail and Chari, bringing Tina along with them, her little feet pattering on the wood. Pity drifts in their smiles.

"You need to get the link checked Bari. We're worried about you."

He can barely hear what Kamail is saying. He's heard the word deluded so many times, he barely understands it anymore.

He slides under the covers, gripping the stone.

And in one breath, it returns to him. His eyes blink open in the dark. He feels her instantly, intensely and overwhelming. Her breath on his neck, her palms floating against his chest. The love seeps in layer after layer, and he hears her. He knows it's impossible, but it feels so real.

"You were worth fighting for." She sobs. His heart jumps in his chest. "I'm sorry Bari. I love you." He feels the danger, the jump of her heart. The words sound like her last, lack of all hope.

"No." He jumps, sweat beading at his forehead. Bari needs to save her. "No, wait." Tears run down his cheeks. "I'm coming."

6

HE RELIVED HER

one

There was so much pain in these four white walls. Adil had to turn his head every time he came across a frame with a picture of them sitting on his oak shelf, the same frames they'd bought together in the dirt-cheap thrift store down the pebbled road. It had been too long to unwrap whatever emotions he had locked under the layers in his mind in a dark, tattered box. One locked so tight that it would be impossible to open no matter how many metaphorical metal crowbars he would use.

He had no good reason to be back here, no valid excuse to roam the streets where she'd once tucked her icy cold hands underneath the hem of his jumper in midst of the fierce pouring rain, and he'd have to hide his delight and the jump of his heart under a nervous chuckle. Where she slid into his bubble so seamlessly, one could've easily thought the two were meant forever. And they were supposed to be, were they not?

Even after it all, Adil had sundry parts of her thoroughly stitched into the aching walls of his heart. Her gentle touch had inflamed his delicate skin, and somehow, she would not burn out. She had stayed lit, even now.

After all this time, she was still there; here; everywhere.

There had been moments where Adil would let his mind drift off to the smell of her, the delight in her gorgeous laugh and the half moons that sat under her eyes after long nights of shifting in and out of sleep; tangled and hot. Their lips would always find each other, and when Leyla would laugh about it the morning after, Adil would tell her it was to remind them that they were still there. To remind each other that they would always be there. And now, they were confined to small gut-wrenching moments of weakness where he'd sink down into the grey carpet under his feet and make a conscious effort to breathe.

The heavy weight of his head was burdened with all the what-ifs and moments in between where he could've said the right thing.

But none of that mattered now; he was back here, in the city tainted with her presence, for merely a few days.

Here, in this sullen, abandoned apartment, once decorated with fairy lights she'd reach to hang up his t-shirt and audaciously laugh back at him when she was unsuccessful, the golden hues from the swaying candle dancing in her eyes.

He knew where he would go first because before he even made the conscious decision, his feet were dragging him along in their own volition. Adil recognised the scent before his eyes caught sight of the bakery, old and rustic. The same as it always had been. And Adil tentatively digested that part of the fact— that not much had changed since he'd last been here. The roads still missed the few grey pebbles, and the wind still whistled the same melody. Maybe she hadn't either.

Maybe they could still— but he never let himself finish the thought. It was an idiotic one, to say the least.

Adil ordered the apple pie, a shared favourite, and the image of her shoving a fork in his mouth flickered like scenes from a movie. He put his fork down then and waited for his heart to stop beating out of his chest before he ate any more.

Next, he went to the bookstore where she had worked and once again convinced himself he was there because he liked the taste of the oat cappuccino swirling around on his tongue. And the statement seemed perfectly plausible, up until he carefully ran his fingers along all the books he'd shown her; the ones she'd fling wide open and bring up to her nose, telling him how she loved the scent of fresh new books and watched as his face changed into one of perplexity.

Inside this city, he relived her.

And he let himself sleep next to her that night, running his quivering fingers along the line of her stomach, disorientated in how she felt soundly and frighteningly tangible. He never wanted the sun to hit his face the next morning, but alas, it did. Slithering, soft and gentle, the sun travelled down his body, forcing him up and out of the comfort of his silk sheets.

two

Adil spent half an hour before his meeting on the kitchen bar stool, fiddling with new designs as he dipped his spoon into hot oats. He had started this project months ago but kept it hidden from his parents. It's not that they wouldn't approve; they would always approve of his creative projects, but since Adil started working for his father, he had many other responsibilities. Being in Paris gave him some time to himself. Time to work on what he'd been thinking about for months. Something for himself.

It was a gentle walk through the city, beautiful patterns moving through each building like a canvas and the smell of fresh bread on every other street. Adil took it all in, the panelled balconies on the edge of tiny apartments, the brick formations, the rich architecture in every direction he looked. Green trees lined up, bare and stripped for the cold winds of Autumn and bustling crowds in clouds of coats, gorgeous whites and pretty pinks. Adil's eyes fell shut for a moment in tranquil realisation he had missed this city. He had missed the smells, and the feel of the wind on his face but most of all, he missed who he used to be.

Adil knew he couldn't revel in it; knew he couldn't plunge head first into moments too far-fetched; moments he barely recalled, but being back here was in no way a sensible idea. But here he was, spending weeks before his flight convincing himself he was obligated to.

Deep down, when he landed, Adil was playing along with his pretence with a slither of his sanity left and little air in his lungs.

"You like Paris, eh?"

His head snapped down then, where the voice had come from. A frail man lay on the edge of the street, his smile bright and honest. He was sitting, legs crossed, and Adil noticed his shoes, with large gaping holes in them. His hair, streaks of white and grey, was rampant and falling to his shoulder. He was wearing a thin t-shirt, and goosebumps lay on the skin of his arms.

In front of him, a thin mat of fabric spilt onto the street, lines of miniature Eiffel tower keyrings and berets with price tags of cheap ink streaks on paper, slanted and messy. Adil thought it looked like a child's handwriting, a feeble attempt to align the numbers.

"It's lovely," Adil said, smiling back at the man.

"Maybe you like a memoir?" He said in a thick accent.

Adil's heart plunged.

"No."

Adil leaned down, shrugging off his coat and reaching out to the man, wrapping it around him. September in Paris was not usually this cold, but today hit freezing, cold winds and plunging temperatures gliding through the city, and Adil was sure that the man would need his coat more than he did.

When Adil got back up and reached out his arms to steady himself and try not to get pushed and shoved by the people on the busy streets, the man had glistening tears in his eyes and a trembling lip.

"Thank you, my friend," he spoke in a tremor. Adil reached into his pocket then, slipping out a ten euro note and handed it to him.

"It's not much, but I hope it helps."

"Thank you."

The man gripped his hand then and leaned into it. "Bless you."

Adil reached the building on time, stepping into the elevator with a beaming mother and her small child, tugging his pants until he looked down at her. Wide blue eyes stared back at him.

"Bonjour." She chuckled.

Adil waved, and the toddler handed him a lollipop and jumped excitedly, laughing and waving her hands in the air.

"Désolé, she's giving everyone her lollipops today." her mother spoke in a thick french accent.

He chuckled.

"She's adorable," he spoke.

"That she is."

She looked like a little ball of fun, and Adil's mind returned, almost in slow motion, to his cousin's daughter, Sofia. First, he pictured her eyes, and then memories came spilling out at a defiant pace, and he became sombre at the thought. He hadn't seen her in forever. Adil's cousin, Samu, had been his best buddy when he studied in Paris, but they lost contact soon after he moved.

The elevator bell rang, and Adil took out his phone and tried to find his number, waving to the cute little girl with his free hand.

CONTACT: Samu

There it was. He pressed on it, and Samu picked it up in less than three seconds.

"I was waiting for you to call me, brother."

Adil missed his voice. A chuckle escaped him.

"Samu. I've missed you."

"How long has it been?"

"Too long. Are you free today?" Adil said.

"Yeah, I'm taking Sofia to the park in a few. She's all grown now. Join us."

Sofia must be six now. She was four when Adil left.

Two whole years.

The thought felt like chalk in his mouth.

Sofia popped up in his head then. The soft hair on her head that she'd force Adil to run his fingers through as she lay on his lap before storytime. Samu and Habiba had been lovebirds long before uni. They had met in school, fell in love and were married by the time Adil and Samu started uni.

Just after Sofia was welcomed into their family, Adil met Leyla.

"Okay, I have a meeting now. I'll text you afterwards."

"A meeting?"

"I work for Baba now, and he wants me to sort some stuff he left unfinished here."

"And Leyla?"

His heart stung a little at the sound of her name.

"She— we haven't talked."

"But she's here?"

He knew the answer to this because, in the hue of the early mornings, Adil had been compelled to check his phone in search of her number. He found it, his fingers trembling when they pressed the cold screen, and the image of her grew larger. She looked identical in her profile, sitting comfortably on a red velvet sofa, her smile cheeky and pouty, a look he knew all too well. The look she'd give him every time she wanted a sip of his coffee; every time she wanted him to cook her favourite meal. He wondered who else she'd looked at like that, but he had no right.

She was wearing a black dress, wrapping around every curve of her body, latching to her soft glorious skin so thoroughly, that Adil breathed a little harder. On the edge of his fingertips, he had memorised tthe curves of her body, the feel of her skin.

Behind her were two large frames; he recognised them instantly. The picture was taken at a museum cafe called Antonie's in the city's centre, one they had been to countless times. Adil had stopped himself before his actions were unruly and had not dared to scroll up to their messages.

He lied anyway.

"I'm not sure."

"Okay, text me when you're done." He said, and he could hear Sofia screaming 'pringles' in the back.

Adil smiled. "Will do."

He hung up, breathed in, and walked into the room number his father had texted to him.

The meeting made his eyes droopy. Working for his father was interesting for the first few months. All real estate, market data and research about fancy white men buying houses. But Adil was bored. Sitting in this room, nothing had sparked his interest.

"We can also look for architecture professionals. Or even give internships to students who are up for the challenge."

His ears lit up. The conversation steered away from the talk about his fathers' real estate matters, and he hadn't been wholly attentive, but they had been talking about a new line of houses.

Designing was all he ever wanted to do, but he had no real experience.

"I'm actually quite experienced in designing," Adil said; he was thoroughly faking his confidence. His leg trembled beneath the table.

"Aren't you the real estate guy?"

"Yes, but I also graduated top of my class in architecture. Here actually. In Paris."

The white guy opposite him widened his eyes.

"Send some of your designs to my guy. If he approves, you're in."

three

"Are you going to do it?" Samu asked, handing him a juice box. They had found a spot in the park, small dandelions sprouting from the ground around them and Sofia running around with her bright pink shoes in the distance.

"It means I'd have to stay in Paris."

"And why can't you?"

Adil didn't have an answer for that. He didn't know how to answer that, but he knew it scared him. Why wouldn't it?

"Well, let's see. I might not even get it."

"Adi, I've seen your designs. Don't underestimate yourself."

"It means I'd have to leave mama."

And there it was, the guilt. And the treacherous foreboding memories that latched onto it. Leaving this city was a trek for Adil, but coming back was harder.

"I'm sure mama will want you to do whatever makes you happy."

"Oh, I know. That makes it worse; she'll tell me to go."

"Adil, it's about what you want at the end of the day. It's about your happiness. No matter how much you love your parents, you live for yourself. I learned that the hard way."

Samu was referring to Sofia. Sofia was adopted, and when Samu told his parents about this, they disapproved. They ignored Samu and Habiba for months of struggle through paperwork and training sessions and had cut off contact.

But when Sofia was born, they came with smiles and gratitude and a big bouquet of flowers, knocking on their door in congratulations. They had accepted as most parents do. And Samu never mentioned it again, because he didn't care much for grudges. The past was in the past. And that's where it stayed.

"I know that," Adil said.

"Then? What's stopping you from taking the chance?"

Adil knew. But somehow, so did Samu.

This city sketched her soul in every cloud and carried the sweet smell of her with every mellow wind.

"You need to call her."

"I left her. Two years ago, I left her and then ended it with a text. What am I supposed to say to her?"

"Just tell her how you feel."

"I don't know how I feel."

"Have you even told her?"

"Told her what?"

"Why you left?"

Adil shook his head, and Samu's face fell.

"Just call her, Adil. She doesn't deserve to be left in the dark."

And as much as he wanted to pick up the phone and dial her number, he wasn't going to. He didn't know how.

He sat next to Sofia at dinner, and her hazel eyes were lighter when she looked up at him and handed him her chewed slimy apple.

"Want some?" She said.

"Oh my God Sofia please put that back in your mouth." Habiba spoke gently to her child.

"But I'm being kind. Khala might want some."

"And that's very nice of you but if you're going to offer him apples, give him a fresh piece so he can chew it himself. He also has teeth."

"Okay mama."

Sofia did exactly that, reaching her little hands out and handing Adil a new piece from her blue plate.

His heart swelled a little. "Thank you."

"You're welcome Khala."

He took it, and chewed it as slow as she was so she wouldn't feel left behind.

Sofia then demanded Adil play outside with her in the garden, where she had a colourful slide and a swing set. He wanted to head home, but when her little hand reached up and grabbed his finger, he was pulled into the garden and had no choice but to oblige.

So they played for hours until her bedtime, and Sofia wouldn't let anyone read her bedtime story unless it was Adil.

"Don't worry, I'll read her a story and then she can go to sleep. Right, Sofia?"

Sofia nodded happily, bouncing as he picked her up and into his arms.

"Good luck." Samu laughed as he headed upstairs with her head on his shoulder, flailing with little balance.

When he tucked her into bed and slid in with her, she opened the book about Carl the bear in the middle of the story and started to. He watched as she slid the pages, skipping a few everytime and kept looking up at him to make sure he was still paying attention. Two minutes in, Adil himself was intrigued by the story of the bear, but he could tell Sofia was falling asleep with the weight of her head becoming slightly heavier on his chest.

"I missed you a lot Khala. Don't ever go again." She said, shifting and sinking further into his chest.

He ran his hand down her tiny back, and kissed her little forehead. "I won't."

four

When Adil had become sullen and was tired of gawking at the blue sky from his apartment window, patterned with rolling clouds, his fingers lingered on the call button for too long before he thumbed the button too hastily and dropped his phone on the carpet. With each deafening ring, his heart raced.

There was a pause on the line after she picked up, almost like she knew.

"Hello?"

Her voice came back soft and firm.

His heart was beating too fast and too hard, he heard the unforgiving echo in the walls of his head. The melody of her voice was lyrical, and his brain made a hasty decision that was all he needed; just a few seconds of her sweet presence over the line where time finally decided to wait for him.

He clicked the red button, but regretted it instantly.

His regret sat with him that evening as he attempted to scrub the pain off his body in the shower; tried to calm his nerves with searing ginger tea. The burn on his tongue helped him concentrate and send a shaky email attaching some of his best designs that he'd worked on in the past few months.

He addressed the email to Nill Randons assistant, the owner of one of the biggest construction companies in Paris.

Adil heard Samus' voice ringing in the walls of his head. *"It's about your happiness"*

He knew that, but it was much harder to put it into practice.

The phone rang somewhere between three and four in the morning, Adil wasn't conscious enough to squint at the time before his finger swiped right.

"Hello?" He spoke, groggy and sleep-rough.

"I knew it."

She spoke, and if Adil hadn't been awake two seconds ago, he definitely was now. Alert and wide-eyed, he froze. He wanted to speak but his voice was lodged in his throat and was unwilling to budge.

"Adil?" She spoke again.

After years of living without it, his name spilling from her lips in a shaky breath felt angelic. That was a lie. Her voice had always been able to soothe his greatest distresses.

"Leyla." he breathed, and it was a trembling frail attempt at pulling himself together.

"You called me."

Shit.

"I did." He spoke, gently. Inside, his heart was anything but.

"And you're using a french number."

"Yeah— I landed in Paris on Monday."

The pause felt drawn out, and he gulped.

"And you— you didn't tell me?" Her voice was quiet, like she was unsure of herself. And Leyla was never unsure of herself.

"I didn't know— if you'd want to see me." His voice came out wrecked.

"I— do want to see you." And then her hesitation allowed his pride to seep in. Reminded him of how he left things with her.

"I can't."

He hung up, and then Adil wanted to roll up in a ball and force himself to sleep. Of course, he could not. Adil fell asleep eventually, but not before his eyes blinked in the dark for hours, stinging and burning with the thought of her.

He had no right; no right to call her. He knew that if he stayed in Paris, he wouldn't know how to resist the memory of her. There would be no distance keeping them apart anymore. If he stayed in Paris, she would be his.

five

The email came in the morning, when the sun had turned the world a little brighter but not bright enough for Adil to slam the pillow over his head to shelter him and sink into the mattress. So he lay flat on his back, and turned his brightness higher.

Dear Mr Adil Akilan

We were very pleased with your design portfolio and would like to discuss a position for you with our company.

Unfortunately, we cannot offer you the head designer position due to your lack of experience but the position will be available after six months of working with us.

Please get back to us with a date of availability for an initial interview.

Thank you.

He sent a screenshot to Samu.

Samu 7:21 AM:
I knew it. what are you thinking?

Adil expected to be happier, but his mind drifted to Leyla. He didn't know if he could live in this city without her. So he called her again. And this time, he felt the pain sitting limp on the line. He felt the hurt, raw and wounded and right there. This time, she was not warm.

"Adil." she breathed, sharp and piercing.

"Leyla I—"

"Why are you calling me?"

"I'm sorry for before. I do want to see you."

There was a pause, and Adils' heart dropped.

"Okay."

"Are you free tonight?" he asked, hoping with every spec of his being that she was.

"I'm going to Marcels with a few friends, do you want to come?"

"Yes." The word slipped from his lips without hesitancy.

They agreed to meet at sunset, and her voice returned to normal, tender and calm. She sounded familiar again, and Adils chest felt weightless. A wave of relief washed over him, and his shirt was soaked through and through by the time he threw his phone on the bed.

Adil 8:08 AM:
I'll call Baba today, see what he says.

Samu 8:08 AM:
let me know
sofia wants to see you again
come for dinner

Adil 8:09 AM:
i'm meeting ley tn

Samu 8:10 AM:
Incoming call

Adil smiled as he brought the phone next to his ear.

"You what?" Samu spoke.

"I called her."

"And?"

"We're meeting at Marcels."

"And how do you feel?"

"I don't know what to say to her."

"Adil, you know her. When you see her, you'll know what to say. Worst case, call me. I'll come get you.

"Thank you brother."

"Adil?"

"Do you love her?"

"Yes."

"Then thats all thats matters."

When Samu hung up, Adil rang his father.

"Salaam, Baba."

"Salaam, my son. How is it in Paris?"

"It's good to be back. I got offered a job."

"Really? Where?"

"At Randy's."

"The construction company?"

"They offered me an interview."

"Do you want it?"

"Yes."

"Then stay. Take the interview."

"Baba, are you sure?"

"Of course I am."

six

Adil confirmed an interview slot at 2pm.

He went to the art museum down the road, the one he'd been eyeing since he walked past it yesterday and saw a hint of gorgeous colours spring out at him. He tucked his white t-shirt into his khaki pants, wore his leather jacket over it and left his apartment with ease. Adil hadn't been to an art gallery in years, and he came to the realisation he'd not done anything for himself in years.

When he caught sight of the one mosaic, blue and purple shades spread all over the piece, he realised he had been here before. He felt a soft kiss on his cheek, and it was Leyla's swollen lips on his. Her small hand wrapped in his, their fingers intertwined. Their tipsy laughs throughout the night.

The memory became dark, eerie and edged with pain. It was the night he asked her to come with him; to leave Paris with him. Their faded agonising voices echoing through the corridors. It came back to him in a sick sort of way, on a leash attached to love and despair, constantly pulling him side to side and leaving him with a queasy feeling at the base of his stomach.

But Adil didn't run away. Not this time. He looked at the paintings with concentration, all the colours and textures and hope sketched into them. He loved being there, alone but not lonely and the colours brought him back to himself. He was conflicted, and he had her memory in his head, but somehow at that moment, he felt okay. Like everything would be okay.

His interview was with a lady named Andy Rosa in one of the old buildings a brisk walk away. She was a petite woman with dark skin and black eyes and long braids with light brown highlights, and small tattoos all over her arms.

"So, no experience huh?" she spoke, opening his file in front of him.

"No, but I'm a quick learner."

She paused, looking down at his portfolio.

"May I ask why?"

"Why what?"

"You graduated and left Paris two years ago, so why haven't you had experience designing?"

"I went back home and worked in real estate for my father. He needed the help."

"Ah, but you're moving back?"

"Well, I guess that would depend on the outcome of this interview."

"Oh, the job is yours if you want it. My boss made that very clear before I got here."

Adil chuckled.

"I do. I just have a few things I need to sort out first to make my decision."

"That's fine. We have a designer leaving us in two months, so you can get back to us in the next month with a definitive answer."

"Thank you."

She moved her arm to pick up her glass of water and Adils eyes landed on an abstract tattoo on her forearm. It was the face of a woman in a line drawing.

"May I ask what this represents?" he asked, his finger gliding to her arm.

She smiled.

"It represents the first woman who ever bought a house I designed. The first woman I loved."

"That's beautiful."

"Do you like art?" She asked.

"Well, I didn't appreciate it enough before, but now, yes."

"What changed?"

"A girl."

She chuckled. "Oh, it always is."

Adil tried not to feel the growing excitement at the thought of this job. The thought of being inspired everyday.

What he didn't expect was for the idea of it to be shut down so quickly.

"Baba, what's wrong?" Adil spoke over the line.

"Your mother."

"What? What happened?"

"I had to take her to the hospital."

"Is she okay?"

"She'll be okay, I think. The doctors are looking at her now. I'll keep you updated."

"Are you okay, Baba?"

"I'm worried, but I'll be okay."

He knew what his father needed to hear at that moment, so he lied through gritted teeth.

"I didn't get the job, so I'll be coming home in two days."

And just like that, it was gone. All the excitement, all the hope.

For a second, he thought if it was even worth it to go see her tonight. And he sat on the edge of the bed and let the thought settle. The mattress sank along with his heavy heart.

But alas, he convinced himself he was stupid not to see her. Not to feel her presence one more time. He convinced himself there would be nothing between them anymore, no pain to relive. Nothing to love. But Adil knew the lie would come back to haunt him because Adil knew, with no ambivalence, that he was still in love with her. And with all the girls his mother had encouraged him to get to know back home, he had refused to go. It was wrong when his heart belonged to another, was it not?

seven

Adil got to the bar with ten minutes to spare, knowing she would be late. She always was. She once told him, under the sheets where they lay tangled and lined with sweat, that she did it purposely so the anticipation of seeing her would soar. So that he would hold her that much tighter when she threw her arms around him and chuckled when he lifted her from the ground.

"Hey, stranger."

He froze, his head snapping back. He met her eyes first, and the glowy tint in them sparkled. She was alone, but he didn't notice that until she spoke. Her face hadn't changed; she was still gorgeous, happy, and full of love.

Still her.

"Hi." he breathed, his voice barely above a whisper.

"I came early, thought we could talk."

All he saw was her, and his teeth were chattering in the caves of his mouth. She was still far from him, but her burning eyes; oh, her eyes brought her infinitely closer. He knew he had to be the one to come to her. She smiled, her smile lines deep. It was ploy that he fell right into.

When he did finally inch closer and wrap his arms around her waist, he pulled her in so tight, he was afraid she would crumble in his arms. When she closed her fist around the back of his neck and squeezed, a flurry of goosebumps travelled down his spine. When she laughed a throaty laugh into the nape of his neck, he wanted to cry. Time blended with each exhale, each movement of her chest against his and by the time he finally let go, he didn't know how long they'd hugged.

They sat on the sofa, with enough distance between them to be cordial, but all Adil could wish was to scooch closer and bring her closer. All he wanted was try and comfort her in all the ways he hadn't been able to in the last two years. All he wanted was for her to let him love her.

He knew the other shoe would drop, and it did.

"Why— why did you come back?" She spoke, and he recognised the pain in her voice. It was a reflection of his own.

A ball of uncertainty lodged in his throat, and pain flickered in his heart.

"I had some business here. My father wanted me to look into some properties."

"Oh."

"How's art school?" Adil spoke.

She chuckled then, and gazed at him, brown hues in her eyes sparkling.

"How did you know?" she said.

"Well, you always wanted to."

She stayed quiet, and it gnawed at his emotions. "It's been two years, Adil."

He knew it was coming. What he didn't expect was for her to say it so blatantly, infused with so much hurt. Adil was off the deep end, and his eyes went to her trembling fingers.

"Leyla, I—"

"Why didn't you come back?"

He noticed the damp accumulating in her eyes then, and his heart split open. He had to tell her the truth, because she saw right through him.

"I was ashamed."

"By what?"

"For all of it. It was selfish to ask you to come with me."

"No Adil. It wasn't selfish to ask. It was selfish for you to expect me to. And then get angry when I refused."

"I know."

"It hurt me too, but I— I thought you'd come back" she spoke, all gentle and melodic, but the pain was there in the air, clawing at the towering wall between them, raw and exasperated. He felt the effect of it stinging in his eyes.

"I'm so sorry—"

He was interrupted then, by a loud pitch scream gravitating toward them.

"Leyla." The girl squealed, and Leyla jerked and faked a smile as she reached up and hugged her.

Her friends followed one by one, and soon, there were six of them sitting around the sofa. Adil managed to laugh at their light humorous energy and felt a sprouting happiness in his chest to see Leyla so happy. He took the time to gaze at her, her long brown locks falling longer on her lap, coiling at the ends. Her smile, wide and free. His eyes travelled to every inch of her, and then retreated to the distance when she'd catch his eye.

eight

When most of her friends were tipsy enough not to notice, a few perched by the bar and the rest swaying gently to the faded pop, Leyla moved closer to him. So close, he felt the warmth radiating off her skin. She smelt like lavender, and home.

"I missed you." she said, and then settled into his chest. He was sure she could hear the fierce beating of his chest, but leaned into her anyway. He couldn't help it. He knew this was not a good idea, not to bathe in her; the way she felt against him, but the moment she glanced up at him, his self control seeped into the air and slithered away from him.

"I missed you too." He whispered, and rested his hand against the slots of her waist.

They breathed each other in for a few comfortable minutes, and then she spoke.

"I'm mad."

Adil knew it was the alcohol talking, but his stomach dropped anyway.

"Why?"

She shifted, and her eyes met his. "You left me. You left me all alone in this dumb city and you didn't give me an explanation."

"I— I know. Leyla—"

"No. You know what? I would have been willing to do long distance for you, but instead, you decided that we weren't worth it."

"No, I never thought we weren't worth it. We are worth it."

She jerked in his arms and her eyes grew wider.

"We are." he said again, reaching for her face. She melted in his hands.

"When do you go?" she spoke, her eyes falling shut as he rubbed his thumb against her jaw.

"Two days." he spoke, solemnly.

"Two days? That's it?"

He nodded, and stared at her big brown orbs. Leyla was tipsy; he could tell by the swaying of her body when she got up and reached out her hands for him to grab ahold of.

"If two days is all we get, we might as well dance."

So they danced, and he got lost in it. The soft sway of her hips against him. The way she melted into him, decadent and becoming. Her arms tight around his neck, no air in the space between them. Just her and them and once again, Adil felt alive. In the graceful feel of her body against him, Adil felt two heartbeats flush and synchronise and he had to clench his fingers around her waist tighter in case this was all a pretence he had manufactured in the profundity of his mind. After she leaned impossibly closer to him and her eyes gazed into his, with a hint of chocolate and tenderness, he was sure of one thing. He loved her, like he would love no one else.

Later, when the bartender had gotten tired of their mishaps and ushered them out, she gravitated towards him. It took Adil right back to blurry nights after long days of uni where her tongue tasted like coffee and alcohol and she would perch up, wrap his large coat around her and demand that they ditch the bar and watch the moonrise. He could never say no to the glint in her eyes and the excitement in her bones.

From habit, his hands found the small of her back and guided her towards the door. The city at night was a breath of fresh air. Twinkling lights in the distance and a flurry of people, lively and kinetic.

One by one, her friends wobbled towards the taxis that Adil had hauled for them, and alas, it was just the two of them again. Her place wasn't far, so he silently agreed to walk her home.

She was deep in thought when Adil glanced at her, and the bottle of emotions he was trying to contain burst open. He pulled her close, and she felt warm against him; comfortably tucked into him like a book on a shelf. She smiled then, slowly swaying and his stomach started doing backflips.

Adil stilled in the middle of the street; his legs wouldn't move. He had this sudden overwhelming feeling to just look at her. To watch as she realised he wasn't by her side anymore and to watch as she spun to find him. And when their eyes met, it was like the first time all over again.

nine

She was wearing a satin red crimson dress that day, the day they'd met; it wrapped around her like a birthday gift. Samu and Habiba were exploring the records from the 80s on the aisle opposite to Adil in the record festival they'd been planning on going for weeks, and that's when she caught his eye. She had her fingers running along a record, over the lines and patterns of the art cover. She was so focused, she hadn't noticed him staring. Which he was, unashamedly. The record festival ran twice over two weeks, so Adil hoped he would see her again.

He wasn't someone to approach a girl just because she was pretty. Which Leyla was. Some might even describe her as gorgeous, with her long locks of brown and hazel and her slight olive skin.

Adil was right. Two weeks later, he saw Leyla again. This time, she was not wearing a dress. Instead, she was buried in a grey oversized hoodie and matching tracks. Her hair was in a bun, and there were two silver chains around her neck and large hoops from her ears. Her face was glowy with not a drop of makeup. It made Adil laugh, the contrast of her appearance.

She caught him staring this time, but merely looked into his eyes and smiled. Then, she turned away and walked towards the live music show. He watched from a distance as she swayed to the light music, and then when the band asked if anyone had musical talent, Samu had shouted, grabbing everyone's attention and urging Adil to go up on stage. He was a mediocre guitar player, but he sat on that stool, trembling, and picked up the chords quickly. As he played, she had her eyes trained on him. And when he caught hers from the crowd, she raised her drink and nodded. One song in, she raised her hand and asked if she could sing.

So they performed together. And his fingers on the strings of the guitar picked up pace, and confidence. With her beside him, he felt like he could do anything.

"You weren't bad, you know." she said.

Samu and Habiba had left to put Sofia to bed, but Adil stayed. He didn't want to admit it then, but he stayed for her. At the tiny chance he could talk to her. He was standing on the edge of the stage, and the festival was almost empty. She approached him from behind, and he could smell her sweet perfume. It was an idiotic thing to think then, but Adil wanted to smell that scent forever.

"I could say the same about you."

And that was the beginning of them. The two lit a spark in each other they weren't able to put out, but with it, a sense of calm and tranquillity. They became best friends first, and shared coffees and brunches and sleepy nights trying to finish the entire list of marvel movies. They failed spectacularly, because Leyla would fall asleep in Adils arms, out cold in mere seconds. She would tuck her head into his neck and wrap her small arms low around his waist, wrapping her fingers around his hips and fall into a sleep so suddenly, all Adil could do was fall asleep too.

It was not until later that Adil realised he was completely in love with her.

He still was, even now. Two years away from her, and nothing had changed.

Now, under the moonlight, she looked back at him with the same eyes. The same smile. The same glowy tint dancing on her face and most importantly, the same sun in her soul, lighting up the world.

He inched closer and placed his scarf around her neck, tying a knot in the front and giving it a little tug. She whispered a sincere thank you, too close and too breathy in his ears to be pragmatic.

Adil tried to focus on the flickering street lights or the sinister silence on the tiny roads but when Leyla reached for his hand and wrapped their fingers together, something ignited in him, and he was not able to douse it.

He was not able to do anything; there was no self control; no self preservation when she leaned in outside her apartment door and placed her soft lips against his without warning. There was a pause; a small moment where time prickled at the skin on his body; where his chest stopped heaving and his lips didn't know how to move. Then, the kiss quickly became familiar and he found purchase in her alluring curves and turned his head, allowing him all of her. There was no going back; not after they had kissed till their lips were swollen, shrugging the clothes of each other's body and moving around the walls like starving animals.

He was not in control when she tugged the shirt from his body, and kissed along the lines of his chest. He felt all her love in the sounds she made when he placed his lips along her jaw, and then down into the depths of her neck. Then, he smelt the light alcohol on her breath and he froze in place.

ten

"What?"

He pulled away from her.

"What is it, Adil?" She said again, reaching out for him.

"I don't want to do this unless you're sure."

"In the last two minutes, what about me wasn't sure?"

He leaned into her, placing his hands around the sides of her neck, touching her forehead with his.

"You're drunk."

"No. I'm not."

"Ley."

"Adil, I promise you I'm not."

"Stand with your leg up for one minute."

Her face fell.

"Are you kidding?"

"Nope."

Adil had made her do this before. She failed. She fell in less than five seconds, and laughed when Adil caught her. Adil put her to bed that night, placing his shirt over her head so that it would smell like her, and tucking her under his covers. That was the first night she whispered 'i love you' into his neck and hummed and then started snoring, all in the same ten seconds.

She rolled her eyes and looked straight into his eyes as she placed her one leg up while Adil took out his phone and set a timer. The one minute gave him a moment to glance at her apartment. How the white vases she said she wanted to paint were covered in floral patterns of rosy pink and baby blues. How there were several more paintings hung up, some with her signature at the bottom. How every small thing he hadn't noticed before was now screaming at him, reminding him of all the changes he wasn't a part of.

One thing caught his eye though, and his mouth fell open.

It was a painting of them, not one anyone else would recognise, but he did. Of course, he did. It was a yellow painting, with their faces in the distance. They were holding each other, close and privy and gorgeous. It was a painting from a picture they had taken in a museum but Leyla had changed the background into a forest. Towering green trees and soil on the ground, beautiful flowers growing on the sides, falling off the edge of the canvas. It was ethereal.

He knew she painted it after he left her, and tears pricked at his eyes.

"You like it?" she spoke gently after the beeping stopped, his phone reminding him it had been a minute. He ignored it, so she reached past his shoulder and pressed the 'stop' button for him.

He had no words, so he just looked at her, hoping she could see that he did. That he didn't like it. He loved it, and her. In her eyes, she spoke all the words he didn't know how to say. And then she stood on her tiptoes, grabbed his face and kissed his forehead.

"It's been a minute, and I didn't fall and I'm not drunk. So are you going to just stand there or are you going to kiss me?"

He did. He reached down and kissed her so hard, she almost stumbled backward. And then he gently pushed her back into the wall behind them, and she fisted his shirt closer and pulled it off him, her fingers then trailing a burning line across his back.

"Are you sure?" he spoke, breathless and panting.

"I'm past sure, Adu."

She pulled his body toward the bed, and they fell together, all tangled and combined. Adil felt out of depth as he sank into her, all the pain and rue dissolving with each movement. She clutched him so tight, it was almost as if he never left.

Almost.

eleven

"Why did you leave, Adil? The real reason." She asked later, when they were both spent and satiated, her head laying on his damp chest and her leg wrapped around him. Her fingers drew lulling circles on his chest while she waited for a reply.

He didn't know how to lie to her.

"My mum was sick."

She jerked against him, her dilated eyes searching his face.

"What?"

"I didn't tell you, because I didn't know how to face you after the fight."

"So when you left, you knew you weren't coming back?"

"No, when I got there, I realised she was worse than I thought. When I knew I had to stay, I sent that text."

"And your mum?"

"She got better, but there are still a few scares."

He saw the tears in her eyes, how she folded her eyebrows and it left him defeated.

"I wish you'd told me." she spoke then, soft and sombre.

"What would have changed?"

"It would've changed a lot of things."

"I think when I expected you to come with me, I didn't even think of a reality where you didn't. I was torn." Adil whispered.

"You just found out your mum was sick, you weren't thinking straight." She turned her head from him.

"Don't defend me, Leyla. What I did was wrong. I screamed at you. I hurt you, and it hurts me everyday."

"I know. It hurt me too."

He smiled then, drinking her sullen eyes in. He was an idiot to ever have let go of this. Leyla placed her warm hands against his chest then, sinking into him.

"When do you go?" she asked, muffled into the nape of his neck.

"You already asked me that."

"I know."

"Tomorrow."

He felt her despondent sigh against him, and it was like a splinter in his heart, digging at his sanity and plunging him into a dark hole he would never recover from.

twelve

Adil spent the morning packing in his apartment, and Leyla watched him, laughing with her cheeks at how he folded his shirts. She sat opposite him on his bed, throwing pillows to distract him, and when he would pin her under him and she'd squeal, he'd delight in the sounds that came from her mouth. He'd kiss her neck afterward and she squirmed beneath him. When she kissed him back, her lips felt like heaven, clenching at the strings of his heart.

Their eyes met, and Adils mouth moved on its own terms.

"For every night you weren't next to me, I slept beside you anyway. For every part of me I left here, a part of you came with me. Leyla, you lived in the walls of my head like a demanding voice that did not settle."

After she'd slept beside him for hours, the early morning orange reflected in her wet eyes as she sat astride him. It was his turn to hold her then, her body heavy and shaky with the weight of her sobs.

"Don't leave." She whispered into his neck, and he hated himself then. Hated himself for it all. He wanted to sink into oblivion.

She had work, so he dropped her there and made sure she was in the building before he walked in the other direction, waving at her in her long beige coat and her beret.

He knew vaguely where the building was, but his horrible sense of direction did him no good.

He found it eventually, after asking a stern old men who didn't know any english. After Adil struggled in French, the man rolled his eyes and pointed to the building.

"Hi, can I see Andy Rosa please?" He asked the assistant, who had piercing blue eyes when she looked up at him.

"Do you have an appointment?"

"No, but I was hoping I could get some of her time to discuss a job I got interviewed for."

"Let me check her schedule."

"Thanks."

After twenty minutes, Adil finally sat opposite Andy's empty chair and realised he was afraid to say this out loud, afraid he'd sound stupid to pass up an opportunity like this.

"Adil, hi." Andy spoke as she entered.

He got up, hugging her.

"Sorry to bother you, I know you're busy."

"No worries, this is Malina, my girlfriend." Andy gestures to a tall woman standing beside her, with long curly brown locks and fair skin. She reached to shake his hand and smiled.

"Nice to meet you."

"Same to you."

She turned to Andy.

"I'll see you at home?"

Andy nodded and leaned in to kiss her.

When Malina left, Andy took her seat in front of Adil, gleaming.

"You look happy," he spoke.

"I'd be happier if you gave me good news right now but I'm guessing if you came all the way here, it's not going to be good, am I right?"

He gave her a sad smile.

"I know this looks stupid." Adil said.

"It does."

"I can't."

"I want to say I understand but I really don't."

"I'm not sure I can explain it to you."

"Okay, look. Whatever is keeping you from this opportunity, you have a month to overcome it and work for us."

"Are you saying you're rejecting my rejection?"

"That's exactly what I'm saying."

Adil chuckles, and Andy shakes her head at him.

"I want you to work with us. You're talented, kind and I feel truly deep down, something like this is what you want. And I can assure you if you do decide to work with us, you will be promoted in less than six months."

"I don't care about the promotion."

"I know. That's why I want you. You do it because you love it. But it's my job to convince you with materialistic manipulations anyway."

She pauses then, and looks right at Adil. It scares him a little, the way she looks at him. Like she can see right through him. Like his best friend is looking at him.

"Can I ask you something?"

Adil nods.

"Does it have something to do with that girl?"

"A little." he lies, and Andy raises her eyebrows. "Okay, yes. But it's not just that, it's a lot of things."

"I understand it's a difficult situation. But if life puts an opportunity on your plate, you usually leap out for it. Even if there's obstacles. Just think about it, Adil. Really truly sit with how you feel."

So Adil did. He took Andy's words and let them settle in the corners of his mind. He thought about it, until he decided.

thirteen

"I get it. I do, and if you want to go back, I'll even help you pack. But if there's one part of you that's telling you to stay, you need to listen to that part." Samu spoke over the phone.

"But they need me."

"Adil, what is it? What is the real reason?"

"I feel guilty for leaving them. Mama is in the hospital, waiting for her son to come home."

"And?"

"And I don't know how to be with her and not be haunted by the past."

"Adil, I know your parents are one of the most important things in the world, but they've lived without you before. They can do it again. If you ask me, it's fear. It's love and fear and they're both combined and eating at you."

"So now what?"

"Do what your heart tells you to do. Listen to you; to what you want. Because that gut feeling that you've been ignoring for so long. That's your self care screaming at you."

There was so many reasons to stay, Adil knew this. But it was the hardest decision he had to make.

"Okay, I'll take today to figure it out."

"Okay. I need a favour. Are you free right now?" Samu asked.

"I'm meeting Ley in a while but yes, I'm free till then."

"Can you pick up Sofia from school? I would but I'm stuck at this meeting with one of my clients."

"Of course."

When Sofia ran out of school, her little head spun and her face saddened, quickly realising her father wasn't there to pick her up. And then she saw Adil, and she screamed so loud, the kid behind her flung back in terror.

She ran into his arms and he threw her up and into the air.

On the walk back, she put her hand into Adils and asked where they were going, looking up at him with her large brown eyes.

"We're going to pick up Khalu Ley. Do you remember her?"

Sofia shook her head, and it broke his heart a little. The four of them were quite close before he left, and Samu had told him that he had reached out to Leyla soon after they broke up.

She said she couldn't be close to them anymore, it hurt too much. Adil understood, of course.

They picked Leyla up, and she kneeled down to greet Sofia. Although she turned her head away after she got up, Adil could see the layer of dampness in her eyes. It hurt her too. And he fell a little more for her right then. The sadness didn't linger in the air for long though; Sofia grabbed both their hands and forced them to swing her into the air. Then they went for ice cream in the park, and Leyla rubbed her hand across the little girl's back after she wailed, falling over at the park.

"It's okay Sof, let it all out."

Sofia wrapped her hands around Layla's neck, until finally, she stopped shaking. There was a tiny scratch on her knee, so they went to Leyla's to hunt for a plaster. Sofia stood in the middle of her apartment, spinning around and jumping up and down.

"Can we keep her?" Leyla spoke into the phone after they'd all sat down on the sofa and put Frozen on her TV as Sofia threw all her chewed up grapes back into the fruit bowl.

"Oh hi Leyla, been a while. And I'm assuming you're referring to my little demon child?" Samu said through the phone.

"Hi Samu. Yep. She's like a little ball of fire."

"It's because they have the same brain age." Adil spoke and that earned him a punch in the arm and a smirk from Leyla. He laughed as she sank into his chest.

"Look, just bring her home before seven. And then we can all have dinner before you leave, Adil."

"Okay, deal."

"And guys?"

"Yes." She said.

"I'm happy for you."

They looked at each other then, and Leyla smiled.

"But if you lose my child, I will murder the both of you."

"Bye samu."

She hung up, and they both stared at little Sofia with her mouth wide open when Olaf waddled onto the screen. They looked at each other, and Adil burst first. He sank into her shoulder, his body heavy with his laughter. She placed her hand around his neck and pulled him in, kissing his forehead. And then his lips. She tasted like grapes and love.

Samu had insisted they stay for desert, so by the time they got back to Leylas, both of them were too full to move. They lay on the sofa, her head against his chest and his fingers running along her scalp.

"I think I need to go." he said quietly. She shifted against him.

"Home?"

"No."

"Then?"

"Home is here, with you. But I think I need to go back to my parents."

"I know."

"I got a job."

"What job?" She asked.

"Randys"

"But thats--"

"Here."

There was a pause before she spoke again.

"You're not taking it?"

"No. I can't."

"Oh."

"But I want to."

"Adil, why are you telling me this? If you're just going to go anyway, why are you giving me hope?"

"Because I want you know I want to."

"Sometimes, wanting isn't enough."

They didn'tt say anything else, just fall and shift against each other through the night, his lips finding hers whenever he wasn't sure she was there anymore. And he realised, with their fingers intertwined and their breath mingled that she was right.

Wanting wasn't enough.

fourteen

Adil was late to the airport; she wouldn't let go of him. He told himself he was going to save his sobs for the aeroplane, but when the tears rolled down her damp, cold cheeks as he held her, he broke. It shattered him, leaving pieces of himself on the floor scattered, out of reach.

All he could think about was the fight before he left her first. And sorrow and despair sprung around his heart.

"Adil, I can't come with you. I have a whole life here. I have plans."

He was horrible, selfish and hurt. "So what now?" he said, disdainfully.

"Adil, I can't decide that. I can't decide that for us." She spoke and reached out for him. He didn't lean into her touch.

It stung, like a brimming pile of emotions, poking and prodding at his heart. He was being cold and withdrawn and he was well aware of it. He was well aware he was hurting her.

"I'm going for a while."

"Okay. We'll work it out okay? We'll be okay."

He sucked his teeth then, and backed away when she tried to reach out for him. The air wouldn't reach his lungs, and the thought of life without her was suffocating.

"I can't Leyla, I have to go. I can't do this anymore, I can't be around you." He screamed, anger swiftly escaping him.

Shock folded her eyebrows; she looked crushed.

He left then, went to his apartment and packed the remainder of the suitcase he had originally left for her. While he packed, he cried. Tears of hurt, palpable and copious and for so long, he didn't know how to stop. He cried on the way to the airport, when his father picked him up in their red family truck he used to pretend to drive when he was a child; it seemed smaller now. He cried silently at night, his mother frail and weak laying next to him.

They would talk sporadically, but he would flounder to maintain his reason when she spoke gently over the phone as if to soothe him.

After a few weeks, when his mother was showing no signs of getting better, he knew what he had to do. There was so much regret in his trembling fingers as he typed out the message.

Adil 1:09 AM:
I'm staying here, so I think it's best if we don't do this anymore.
I love you, Leyla.

She called after that, thirty-six times. Adil didn't pick up.

She called him everyday after that, until she didn't. He meant to call her back at some point, but his guts would fold inside out every time he thought of the hurt in here voice, and he would flip the phone on his grey sheets and slam his head against the pillow. Adil tried not to cry, but most nights, a burning tear would drop down his cheek and remind him of all that he lost to be here.

And now he was going back, dragging his suitcase down the marbled floor to check in. Back to leaving her behind. The only thing he ever wanted.

His phone buzzed. It was baba.

"Everything okay?"

"Yes, all is fine. Adil?"

"Yes?"

"Why did you lie to me?"

"About?"

"The interview you took. You got the job, didn't you?"

"I don't— I don't want you to think I don't care."

"We know you care about us, Adil. We know you love us. But we want you to be happy."

"I am happy being close to you."

"Not as happy as you are in Paris."

"Baba no I—"

"Son, I cancelled your flight. Stay."

"Wait, baba."

"No, I refuse to deny you your happiness. Our only job as parents is to make sure your soul is good. And Adil, you got yours from your mother, as light and bright and as selfless as an angel."

He heard his mothers voice then.

"We know you love us. Look after yourself, okay? And come visit us. We will welcome you with open arms. And Adil?"

"Yes mama?"

"Keep her happy."

"Who?"

"Hey stranger." She spoke, and her voice fluttered through him. She felt like hot ginger tea on a biting winter day. She felt like everything, all the love, admiration and passion all at once. He spun and froze in time.

She was holding a bouquet of roses, and wrapped in the same red crimson dress as she was the first time they'd met. Hoops dangled from her ears and her smile was wide. There was still a layer of damp in her eyes and small bags underneath them from a few hours ago but she'd done a good job in covering it up.

She inched closer then and reached for him, and he placed his arms around her.

"These are for me." She said, pointing to the roses.

He laughed.

And once again, Adil basked in her warmth, the way her chest moved against him, the way her hands found purchase in the dips in his back.

They went to the bakery then, and all the scenes he imagined a few days ago became reality, with their fingers intertwined and their love scenting the air of every street they wandered. Then, they went to the bookstore and this time, Adil loved the smell of fresh books too. Finally, they went home to his apartment. And it was sullen no more. Now, it had been tinted by all her little habits. She stood on the chair and he stood below her, reaching out his arms to steady her as she hung the fairy lights across the window sill.

"Good?" she asked.

"Great." he spoke, and she looked back with a spark in her eyes.

Then, her foot slipped and she fell backward. She gasped and flung into him but Adil was quick to react and caught her before she hit the floor, wrapping his arms tight around her.

She laughed, and it sounded sweet. He laughed too. And in her laugh, he found forever.

He would sink into the depths of her warmth every morning and he'd make up for his absence every night under the moonlight. He'd never let go again. And Adil relived her, everyday for the rest of his life. He relived her, through the bright hues in the clouds and the melody of the wind and every spec of soil in this city.

He relived her. Forever.

7

ZARIA

The petal landed on his open-toed shoe, brown and wilted. Milo sighed, bending to reach for it and placed it in the centre of his palm. The petal was drooping and folding into itself and had lost all its once vibrant colours. Milos' lip trembled and his heart sank in his chest. He breathed a sigh and closed his door as he entered the bustling streets of the market.

The beam of light was duller today, not by a lot. It wasn't evident to anybody but Milo. His eyes travelled to the sky where the beam led to, fading between the clouds. The other half of Zaria wasn't visible today, the tops of trees, hidden under layers of fog. Every now and again, he saw the glow of fairy wings, hard at work to keep the beam alive.

The ground shook beneath him, and the crowd stopped for a few seconds while the grumbling spread out miles across the city and into the fields. Soon enough, once the danger had subsided, the crowd resorted back to their usual antics, choosing their next piece of jewellery, and purchasing new rugs for their freshly built houses. Everywhere he looked, he saw a Zarian with a fairy, hand in hand walking along the market. Few who didn't have fairies had a pet, a troll or a gnome. Zarians never liked to be alone.

Milo walked past the crowds and into the floating rock forest. As usual, he wanted nothing but peace, and the only place he could find it was deep in the forest, where the soul of the planet of Zaria lay. When he reached the beam, he sat on the grass beside it and breathed in, the air flowing into his lungs. With his hand just below his chest, his stomach contracted.

"Feel her breathe. Make it your own." Milo heard his grandfather's voice echo around him. "This is how you harness her power. This is how you help her."

Only a blanket of dark enveloped behind his closed eyelids, but he felt her. He felt Zaria churn at her core, and he felt her anger erupt into him. All her warning signs crept into him like a spell, and he saw her intentions clear. And then she was calm, and under him, she growled despondently.

When Milo finally opened his eyes, colours slowly came back to him, revealing themselves in waves. First, it was green. The overgrown trees waving with the wind, spreading miles into the distance. Then, yellow. Sprouting flowers in the ground, wilted no more. The beam became bright once again, continuing to power the planet Milo had been protecting since he was a boy.

Suddenly, his breathing turned laborious, and pain shot through his chest.

"You cannot do that for much longer, you know." A voice said from behind him.

His head spun, Lena jumping swiftly from the lowest branch, using her wings to slow her descent. Almond-like eyes stared back at him, big and brown. Her hair reached the tops of her thighs, curly brown locks, glowing blonde under the beam. Her skin was dark and gorgeous, and she had brown circular patches of skin around her eyes. Milo had only seen them glow once, a late night where the two had lay on the grass and watched as the beam dimmed, letting night settle in Zaria

Lena held great power on her side of Zaria, and the glow patches around her eyes helped them set her apart from the rest, lighting up her face when all else was dark, so they knew who she was. Even at night, her power blazed.

"I don't have a choice." Milo groaned, holding his chest, as the pain staggered in waves through his body.

Lena slumped beside him on the floating rock and peered to the lakes below. "What did she say this time?"

"She's angry. Zarians are exploiting her power."

Her face turned into one of anger, lines spread across her face, and she used her wings to lift her off the ground, hovering in front of him.

"You need to tell the head Zarians." She said angrily.

"Lena, you know they won't listen."

Milo was calm, despite her fierce stance against him. A pain shot through his chest, and he doubled over falling to his knees.

Lena worriedly kneeled in front of him. "Milo, it's killing you."

"I'll be fine." He groaned.

She held his face in her hands. "Tell them, or I will."

Milo never liked to admit it, but the head Zarians scared him. There were three men, who controlled the economy of Zaria, and they never hesitated to get rid of anyone who challenged their power

"How?"

"Call for a meeting. Milo, do you think all my fairies work for nothing? For Zarians to kill her soul with their greedy antics."

"No, you know I don't."

"I just don't understand why you're killing yourself to protect them."

"I'm not doing it for them, I'm doing it for her."

"And I'm sure Zaria appreciates it, but if you die, she'll kill them."

"What?"

"You know it's true. She will set this side of the planet into flames if she must. You're the only thing in her way."

Milo closed his eyes. An eerie feeling crept, lifting the hairs on his neck. As usual, she was right.

"Fine."

Lena pushed a strand of hair away from his sweaty forehead. "You can't die. I'll never forgive you."

His lip tugged upward, and he looked in her glimmering eyes, and then at her lips.

"Get up." Lena said, pulling away from him. "And do your damn job."

He smiled as she jumped from the floating rock and used her wings to propel into the air. She didn't look back, but Lena never did.

Milo huffed and sat back onto the rock. He had to tell them, but he needed to do something for himself first.

He sat on the grass, breathed in and out until he felt connected to every fibre of her being. Zaria was humming, and he felt her pain and her love all at once. When Milo opened his eyes, he was reborn.

"I need you to listen to me, she is dying."

The head Zarians scoffed, seated comfortably in their thrones.

"You think we're going to listen to you? The grandson of a madman. Nobody can talk to this planet. Zaria provides for us, that's her job. We use the beam of light to power our entire system. We're not going to stop just because you had a vision of her dying."

"I'm not asking you to stop, I'm asking you to slow down." Milo pleaded.

"No. We will do nothing of the sort."

Milo frowned, placing his head in his hands. "She'll kill you." He whispered.

"Excuse me?"

"She will kill you." He shouted, and the head Zarian grimaced in front of him.

"Take this boy away, before I kill him myself."

Milo struggled as two armed Zarians came from behind him and grabbed him by the arms. They dragged him away, and the punch knocked him out before he could protest.

He stirred awake in a dark, damp metal box. In and out of sleep, Zaria talked to him. She told him stories of a land of peace and possibility. He was pulled back to reality with a familiar flutter.

"Milo." Lena whispered.

Milo groaned, stretching his limbs from the ball he'd formed on the ground. His stomach made a growling noise as he squinted at her.

"Come, we have to go."

She kneeled in front of him and placed her arm around his waist, pulling him toward her. "I'm sorry I told you to do that, it was hopeless."

He smiled at her.

"You knew." She said, "And you did it anyway."

He nodded. "I did it for—"

"I know, I know you did it for her."

"No," he said. "I did it for you."

Lena stared at him and scoffed, but Milo didn't miss the smile tugging at the edge of her lips. "Come on. Let's go before they behead both of us."

Milo chuckled weakly as she lifted both of them off the ground.

Milo awoke in the grass, with Zaria whispering in his ear. Filled with fury, she showed him visions of flames under his eyelids and the ground trembled underneath them.

He turned to see Lena, lying peacefully beside him. She smiled when their eyes met.

"Zaria is not waiting anymore." He whispered.

"I told you."

He huffed. "I guess I'm burning with them."

"No, no way. You're coming with me."

"Lena, no. Zaria needs me here."

"Milo, once the flames start, there's going to be no here. You can talk to Zaria from there." She pointed to the sky, where the other half of Zaria was clear. The tops of trees and forests and floating rocks.

"Lena. This is my life. This is all I've ever known. I can't come with you. No man has ever been to your side of the world."

"Zaria won't spare you. She is powerful and unforgiving."

"How about you trust that she will?"

"But--"

He put a finger on her lip. "Lena, I'm not scared of death."

Her damp eyes glimmered, and her lip trembled. "Milo."

"I promise, I'll be okay."

The idea was far-fetched. Milo probably wouldn't survive the hell Zaria would rain down on them, but in her eyes, there was hope. If Lena had hope, he would too.

The flames came, and fiercely too. Zaria, one by one, burnt the Zarians.

When the flames reached the forest where Milo lay, he closed his eyes and waited patiently for the pain. Trembling, he felt a hand in his.

"It's okay." Zaria whispered. "You're okay."

When he opened his eyes, he saw nothing but colours. He felt himself in every part of Zaria, and he knew then, this was not death.

He felt Lena's pain when the flames subsided as she lay over the ashes, copious tears falling from her cheeks.

"So, you did love me." He said, and Lena jumped in her spot on the charred ground.

She wiped her tears away, touching the ground with gentle fingers. "You—"

"I'm here. I'll always be here, Lena."

She smiled, and he felt her love like a hug.

"She did forgive you." She wept.

Milo smiled, and the grass grew greener, and flowers sprouted from the ground. "She did me one better."

Milo would live among the trees, and float in every cloud in the sky. He would fly with every bird, and smile with every fairy. He would feel Lena's love like no other.

Zaria had given him the gift of eternity.

(the end)

If you got here, it means you liked these stories.
So, I want to say thank you.

I hope you find what you look for in life.
I wish for your safety, your peace and your happiness.
Remember, it's in you.
Everything you hope to find is a heartbeat away.

All you must do is open your eyes to this wonderous world of possibilities.
You must accept the good and the bad and the ordinary.
This is the key to happiness.
Accept your circumstances. And love them as they are.
Through love, you will prosper.

And you will rest.

Printed in Great Britain
by Amazon

47541806R00059